THE SURE HAND OF GOD
Erskine Caldwell

An express train ran over and killed Putt Bowser, and Molly, his blowsy, middle-aged widow took a maudlin swig at her future — *'Nobody wants me. I couldn't hold a man even if one with broken legs fell into my lap'*. But she has to change her mind. She must find a replacement for Putt. Her habit of drinking wine by the gallon has made the financial crisis acute. And when Putt's no-good brother arrives uninvited to pursue her sensation-hungry teenaged daughter, things go hilariously from bad to worse.

ERSKINE CALDWELL

The Sure Hand of God

WHITE LION PUBLISHERS
London and New York

12-9-74 BENTLEY 6.33

First published in the United Kingdom by
Heinemann, 1958

White Lion edition, 1973

SBN 85617 517 X

Printed in Great Britain by
Biddles Ltd., Guildford, Surrey,
for White Lion Publishers,
138 Park Lane, London W1Y 3DD

Chapter 1

MOLLY and Lily went home after the funeral and pulled down the shades in the parlour and had a good long cry together. They sat side by side on the red sofa, tearfully grieving, and thought about what had happened. Molly had a bouquet of yellow and white chrysanthemums somebody had given her at the graveside and she held the flowers close to her face and smelled their fragrance and wondered how she would ever manage to live and pay the rent now that Putt was gone.

'What a life for the female element,' Molly said, wiping her tears on the flowers. 'There's nothing in the whole wide world worse than losing the man you've counted on to support you.' Discouraged and heartbroken, she moaned inconsolably. 'It's a godforsaken shame, that's what it is,' she muttered to herself.

While Lily sobbed softly beside her, Molly stared morosely at a slit of late afternoon sunlight that fell upon the tall blue china vase on the centre table. Tossing the bouquet to the floor, she got up and motioned impatiently for Lily to help her. They pulled and tugged at her girdle and squeezed the roll of flesh around her hips until the girdle finally could be removed. When it dropped to the floor, Molly stepped out of it and gave it a kick that sent it flying across the parlour. Her brassiere had split during all the exertion of getting the girdle off, and she ripped it away and flung it aside. She felt better immediately and the tears stopped running down her cheeks. It always made her feel like a different person when she could go without her girdle and let her body fall into its natural shape. She walked to the other side of the parlour and back, moving her small pudgy hands gratefully over the unconstricted bulging mounds of flesh. Then she sat down beside Lily and picked up the chrysanthemums. She smelled the flowers briefly before crushing them into the hollow of her breasts.

'You're just beginning to know the sorrows of life, honey,' she said as she patted Lily's hand. 'You never had a real father of your own, and now you've lost your first stepfather. It's a godforsaken shame, that's what it is. All you've got in the world now is me—a middle-aged old somebody who's just buried the man I'd counted on to take care of us for the next ten years, anyway. And just look at me!' she sobbed wretchedly. 'Just look at me! Who'd want to marry me now if he could get one of those skinny young widows! My hair won't take a curl and I can't find a girdle that helps my figure and my brassiere won't hold me up and men've got the notion that they can't have the kind of good time they want with widows past thirty-five, anyway. What am I going to do? What's to become of me?'

She stopped and gazed tearfully at Lily. The woeful expression on their faces made both of them begin crying again.

'If Putt had lived,' Molly said, trying to hold back her sobs, 'if Putt had only lived, I was going to reduce and dye my hair a nice deep dark-brown shade—but he's gone now and it's too late!'

She was unable to sit still after that, and she got up and walked aimlessly around the parlour. Presently, as though unable to bear her sorrow any longer, she threw herself against the wall and began beating on it with her clenched hands.

'It's a godforsaken shame, that's what it is!' she wailed. 'Why did it go and happen to me—why didn't it happen to somebody who doesn't deserve a man to provide? And it had to go and happen just after I'd finished working so hard to get him. Putt was a good man, too, even if he was scrawny and weak-looking in the seat of the pants. What am I going to do? What's to become of me now?'

Lily got up and went to her mother. She put her arms around Molly and tried to comfort her. Molly continued to wail and beat the wall with her fists until Lily could take her back to the sofa.

'You can still make yourself look nice, Mama,' Lily told her consolingly. 'You're really not a bit old, and it's not too late. When you get some new clothes and things, you'll look as nice as anybody. I just know you will, Mama. Please don't feel so bad about it.'

Molly's face brightened.

'Do you really truly think so, honey?' she asked hopefully.

'Of course, Mama,' Lily assured her. 'There're a lot of women much older than you are.'

'But I don't know anybody who's cursed with the kind of figure I've got. Just look at me!'

'When you fix yourself up, you look wonderful, Mama.'

Molly smiled for the first time and put her arms under her heavy breasts and pulled herself up. Then she lay back against the sofa and relaxed comfortably.

When Molly married Putt Bowser, he was nearing sixty and she was well past thirty, and most of the women in town were relieved to know that she had gone to live with Putt, because for a long time they had been afraid she was going to succeed in taking one of their husbands. It was a great relief to them in other ways, too. Molly was not the kind who would think of drawing a line between a married man and an unmarried man when it came to the matter of an evening's entertainment.

'If I could have my way,' Lucy Trotter had said, 'I'd run her out of town so fast she wouldn't have time to leave a single track behind. I wouldn't trust her married or unmarried, and I'm going to watch my husband just as close as I ever did. Of all the houses in town, why did she have to move next door to me? It was a mean quirk of fate, that's what.'

Lucy Trotter was one of several married women who continued to be outspoken against Molly long after she had married Putt Bowser and moved into the dilapidated four-room bungalow next to the Trotters. Lucy's husband, Clyde, who owned a small planing mill on the outskirts of the town, was one of the men who had dropped in on Molly when she lived at Mrs. Hawkins' boarding-house, and Lucy had never forgotten that Clyde had a weakness for stout blonde women.

When Molly heard what Lucy Trotter had said about her, she laughed indifferently. 'That's the way they all talk when they can't keep a man home at night,' she had said. 'It's a god-forsaken shame that Clyde Trotter has to be tied down to a scantling like Lucy, though. Clyde's a good man.'

Up until the time Molly married Putt Bowser she had frequently entertained men in the room she and Lily had at Mrs. Hawkins' boarding-house. Mrs. Hawkins, who liked to sit with Molly and have a few glasses of red wine with her, made no objection to the callers as long as they wiped their shoes in muddy weather and did not leave tracks in the hall. As soon as Molly married Putt, though, she moved to the small paint-peeled bungalow they rented on Muscadine Street next door to the Trotters in the West End and settled down to keep house for Putt and Lily.

Lily, who was sixteen and dark-haired with large brown eyes, had grown up to be free and easy in her behaviour, but she was pretty and well-mannered. Boys liked Lily because she never slapped or pretended to be offended, and girls were envious of her because she could stay out with men as late as she pleased and did not have to be home by midnight. Molly had decided that Lily would have her best opportunity to marry when she was young, and she encouraged all men over twenty-one who took the slightest interest in her. Lily had finished the first year of high school when they lived with the Billingses in the lower end of the county, but she had not been to school since, because Molly was afraid going to school almost every day in the week would interfere with her chances of getting married. She wanted to get Lily married and out of sight, because ever since they had gone to live at Mrs. Hawkins', men always became more interested in Lily than they did in her, and it hurt Molly's pride to know she could not compete with Lily's youth and charm.

Molly, who was blonde and extraordinarily plump, always liked to have two or three glasses of red wine before breakfast every morning or she would feel badly and be out of sorts for the remainder of the day. She had acquired the habit of drinking wine from time to time when she worked for Roy Hoey, who ran a lunch room and filling station at Slowdown Crossroads near the Billings' farm. She often had giggling spells that became so violent she lost control of herself and sometimes slid out of her chair and rolled on the floor unless she went to the bedroom in time and lay down until the spasm was over. There was no particular thought that brought on the giggling spells, but sometimes after a few glasses of wine the most casual remark would bring on the first convulsive hic. At other times, even when she was alone in the house, a glance at herself in the mirror would send her off into one of the spasms.

When Putt married Molly, he did not know anything at all about her habit of drinking wine and he soon found out that it was such a drain on his pocketbook that sometimes they had to go without food in order to buy two or three gallons a week. Putt had never known anyone like Molly before and he had never been completely at ease in her presence. He often went hungry after they were married, because after Molly drank two or three glasses of wine, they always had hamburgers with ketchup or hot dogs with mustard for breakfast, another habit she had acquired at Roy Hoey's, and he had never been able to eat hamburgers or hot dogs so early in the morning. Putt did odd jobs down town, such as hauling baggage on his push cart and washing cars at a garage, but the job he liked best of all was carrying the mail pouches from the post office to the railroad station. He met every passenger train, day and night, but it was an easy job because the post office was only on the other side of the courthouse square from the depot, and there were only four trains a day and two at night.

'Putt, you go to a lot of trouble lugging those mail sacks back and forth across the square every day,' Sam Wiggins, one of the storekeepers, told him once. 'I'll bet if you opened up that sack right now all you'd find would be a stack of past-due bills and a bunch of quack medicine ads.'

Putt joggled the pouch higher on his shoulder and rubbed his grey whiskers affectionately against the soiled canvas cloth.

'There's a lot of sorrow in the world, and only a little bit of joy and most of it's right here on the inside of this mail bag,' Putt replied, turning away and hurrying off to the post office.

Every now and then some of the men downtown got together

and thought up a trick to play on Putt, such as the time they rigged up a locomotive whistle on the exhaust pipe of an automobile and fooled Putt into believing a mail train was coming in ahead of schedule, and then everybody rushed over to the depot and had a big time laughing at Putt when he got there all out of breath and discovered that the whistle had been rigged up to fool him.

After all those years, carrying the mail had become a serious matter to Putt Bowser and he said he believed nobody ought to joke about the U.S. mail or the Methodist religion.

A few weeks after being fooled by the whistle on the exhaust pipe, and only a short time after he had married Molly, Putt was crossing the tracks with a sack of mail over his shoulder and was run over and killed by a new fast streamliner called the Morning Sunbeam, which was not scheduled to stop at Agricola. The engineer stopped the train as quickly as he could, though, and backed it up to the station and made out a report of the accident, claiming that Putt was trespassing on the railroad company's property, failed to yield the right of way, and a lot of other things like that. Nobody had much to say at the time, because everybody felt badly about Putt Bowser being run over and killed, no matter whose fault it was, and the shiny new streamliner pulled out as soon as the engineer and conductor finished filling out the report and giving it to the station agent to file at the head office.

People missed Putt more and more after that, because he had known by name every man, boy, and dog in town, and had always had a good word to say to everybody he met going back and forth between the post office and the railroad station. The postmaster had to carry the mail himself for the next day or two, but the day Putt was buried in the Methodist cemetery the postmaster got a light delivery truck to haul the mail and hired a small Negro boy to drive it.

Putt's death was a great shock to both Molly and Lily, but it was especially upsetting to Molly, because for the first time in her life she had become accustomed to having a man support her, and she had looked forward to having Putt provide for her needs. When she and Lily first moved to Agricola from the Billings' farm in the lower end of Cherokee County, where she was Mrs. Billings' housekeeper, she had done a little sewing to help pay their room and board at Mrs. Hawkins', but as soon as the women in town found out that she entertained men, both married and single, in her room at the boarding-house, nearly every one of them stopped giving her any work to do. The only woman in Agricola who still engaged her occasionally for a day's sewing was Christine Bigbee, the Methodist minister's wife, and Christine never sent for her unless Reverend Bigbee was out of town attending a church conference or something of that nature. Each time Christine sent for her, she always reminded Molly to bring the you-know-what. The you-know-what was a small black case that contained a hypodermic syringe and a bottle of vitamin fluid. Molly had bought the outfit from a man who once stopped overnight at the boarding-house and who needed the money to pay his bill. Doc Logan, who had most of the medical practice in town, sold Molly a mixture for the injections at ten dollars a gallon, and she could give nearly a hundred treatments from each batch of vitamin fluid that Doc Logan prepared for her. He had warned her against injecting the fluid into the arteries and had instructed her to give the injections in the fleshy rump of the body. She had been highly successful, particularly with the treatments she gave Christine, who paid her a dollar for each vitamin shot, and up until the time she and Putt were married she sometimes made as much as eight or ten dollars a week. Whenever Molly felt blue or discouraged, she would ask Lily to give her an injection and soon thereafter she was feeling gay and carefree. She had been taking the injections once a week until she married Putt, but after that she began taking one every other day and sometimes oftener, because they made her feel a lot better, and then she drank some wine in between times in order to keep up her spirits.

'Well, he's stone dead in the ground now, and I'm just a middle-aged old widow,' Molly said bitterly, shaking her head slowly while she stared at the floor. 'It wasn't fair to leave me like this, at my age. I can't grow any younger, no matter how hard I try, and everybody knows how men are—they all go for young girls and skinny young widows under thirty-five. Nobody wants to sleep with a middle-aged old widow as big

13

as a ginhouse roof. I haven't got a chance in the world now. I couldn't hold a man even if one with broken legs fell in my lap this very minute. He'd be sure to slide off as slick as he would off a ginhouse roof. I just know he would. It's a godforsaken shame, that's what it is.'

'Papa wouldn't want us to feel like this,' Lily said, brushing the tears from her cheeks. 'He wouldn't want us to blame him too much. It wasn't his fault, Mama.'

'Maybe it wasn't his fault,' Molly said bitterly, 'but I ought to have had the sense to pick out a man who could've dodged a train on a track.'

'Please don't blame him, Mama,' Lily said tearfully. 'He's dead and gone now!'

Molly was silent for a while. The sun had set and the slit of light on the tall blue china vase had disappeared. The room was becoming dark and gloomy.

'He was such a good man—so steady and reliable with his weekly wages,' Molly sobbed in a sudden outburst of feeling. 'Putt always handed me his weekly wages every Saturday night —I can't forget that!' She picked up the bouquet and crushed the flowers between her breasts again. 'I always did get the dirty end of the stick! It's a godforsaken shame, that's what it is!' Her face became flushed with anger and she hurled the bouquet across the parlour. 'Maybe I'll have better luck next time,' she said, her voice all at once rising to a high-pitched giggle. 'If he's a good man and strong in the seat of the pants, it'll make up for everything that's gone wrong.'

Lily jumped up and tried to pull Molly to her feet.

'Come on, Mama!' Lily said anxiously. 'You know how hard it is for you to stop when you start giggling like that. Please come on to bed and lay down.'

Molly got up unprotestingly. 'It's an awful blow to a woman like me,' she said sorrowfully as she looked at Lily. 'I'd noticed it before, but I didn't think it'd happen to me so soon—the Good Lord always takes away the good men first. I don't know why that is, either, unless it's because they're so good they wear themselves out quicker.' She began giggling again, and Lily led her firmly from the parlour and across the hall to her bedroom.

14

Molly stretched out on the bed while Lily was getting the quilts from the closet.

'I was afraid something was going wrong,' she said unhappily as she watched Lily bring the quilts to the bed. 'It was too good to be true. It all goes to show what a hard time a woman has, though. Even if she gets a good man, she can't be sure she's going to keep him. Either another woman comes along and takes him away or else he ups and dies. What a life for the female element,' she said with a deep sigh.

Before Lily could spread the quilts over her, Molly pointed at the small black case on her dressing-table.

'I need the vitamins, honey,' she said desperately. 'We both do after the sorrow we've had. Get the little case and take out the needle.'

Lily filled the syringe and jabbed the needle into Molly's enormous rump. Her body shook with a convulsive quiver when the needle penetrated her flesh, but after the first shock she lay quietly until Lily had pressed the plunger to the bottom of the syringe. As soon as the needle was withdrawn, Molly pointed over the top of her shoulder, indicating that she wanted an injection on the other side of her rump. She lay motionlessly until Lily had finished, and then she got up and refilled the syringe herself. Lily was already shaking her head pleadingly.

'I feel all right, Mama,' Lily protested, backing away. 'Honest, I do, Mama! Please don't do that!'

'Of course you need the vitamins,' Molly said, catching her by the arm and pulling her toward the bed. 'Everybody ought to take them.' She lifted Lily's skirt, at the same time giving her a forward push. 'Don't you notice the difference in me already?' She turned Lily over on her stomach, squeezed the flesh between thumb and forefinger, and quickly jabbed the needle into her. 'You'll feel like you're sitting on top of the world in no time at all, honey.' Still trembling, Lily got up as soon as Molly had pulled out the needle. 'Now, cover me good with the quilts, honey,' she said as she stretched out on the bed.

When Lily had finished tucking the quilts around her, Molly reached out and patted her fondly.

'Don't worry about me, honey,' she said, giggling again. 'I've got my vitamin shots now and I'll be all right. Both of us'll wake up in the morning feeling as cocky as a rooster on a ginhouse roof, in spite of our sorrow.'

Chapter 2

THE next morning Molly got up early and began making black lace step-ins for Lily and herself. She had always been good at doing any kind of fancy needlework ever since Mrs. Billings had taught her to sew, and she was glad to have an opportunity to make something that was both useful and nice looking. Her eyes were still faintly red from crying so much at the funeral, but after three glasses of wine she was calm and her needle fingers were steady. After breakfast Lily came into the parlour where Molly had spread out the patterns she had cut from old newspapers. Molly's tawny thin hair was bound close to her skull with a mass of rubber and wire curlers, and she was wearing her favourite green dressing-gown. It was a skimpy knee-length, half-sleeve rayon jacket that she had made a few days before she married Putt, and it was so comfortable and unconfining and gave her so much freedom that she often wore nothing else from morning until she went to bed at night.

Molly was busily basting a seam when Lily sat down.

'What are you making, Mama?' she asked curiously.

Molly cut the basting thread with her teeth before she answered.

'I'm making some mourning clothes for us, honey. While I was at it, I thought I owed it to you to make something really truly useful. You don't have a single stitch of black underwear, and there's no better time to fix ourselves up than right now.' She bent over her work industriously. 'Everybody knows it's the proper thing for the female survivors to wear some mourning when the man of the family passes away, and black step-ins always do more for a woman's personality than any other kind of mourning I've ever seen. We can't afford to sit around and wait for nature to catch up with us, because there's no knowing how much time that would take, and I'm not in a waiting mood, neither. Besides, the only time nature ever helped me out was when I gave it a good sharp prodding. Every woman ought to keep some black underwear on hand, anyway. You always need it when you least expect it.'

'Are we going to wear black stockings and black dresses, too?' Lily asked.

'Of course not, honey. It's not necessary to go that far.'

'But who'll know we're wearing mourning, Mama. And if nobody knows—'

'The right busybodies will always find out, honey,' Molly said, 'and that's the whole perfect story. Black underwear is like a surprise package, because it makes a man curious to find out what's on the inside. You'll notice how people jerk off the strings and wrapping paper of a surprise package without stopping to undo it carefully like they would if it was only something they'd bought themselves at a store and knew all about. That's the way every last living man is the whole wide world over. Men are always snooping around looking here and there, hoping to find a woman all dressed up in nice black underwear, because if they find it they always think they're getting something done up specially for them. It never makes a bit of difference who the man is, either, because high or low, rich or poor, bashful or brassy, they all behave alike about certain fundamental things. I've known enough men in my time to know what I'm talking about, and that's why I'm making these step-ins for us. You ought to be thankful, honey, that you've got a mama like me who knows what's best to do at a time like this.'

'Are we going to wear black underclothes all the time?' Lily asked.

'No,' Molly told her, bending over her work. 'No, not all the time. Just when we want to make a good deep impression on the right somebody, honey.'

Molly worked on the underwear all day, except for pausing occasionally long enough to drink a glass of wine, and when night came, she was tired and her back ached. Nevertheless, she was highly pleased with what she had accomplished since early that morning. By that time, having had the whole day to think about it, she had decided that the mourning period would soon be over and, since she considered it to be a final finishing touch as well, she worked some pink rosebuds into the hems of the garments.

They tried on the step-ins in Molly's room after supper. Lily's fitted her perfectly, and she was delighted with her appearance when she saw herself in the mirror, but Molly was disappointed. She had made hers several sizes too small and she could hear the seams rip when she tried to fasten the garment around her waist. She knew she could never wear them until she let out the seams and she tried to hide her feelings as long as Lily was there. After Lily had gone to her room, Molly closed the door and took off the step-ins while tears filled her eyes. She had purposely made them several sizes too small, hoping she would be able to squeeze into them some way, but while she was opening the dresser drawer and putting them away she knew she could never wear them until she forced herself to reduce.

Drying her eyes, she went to the mirror and began removing the clips from her hair. She watched hopefully as she removed each clip, but by the time the last one was out, the curls in her thin silky hair began unrolling, and one sweep of the comb took away the last remaining suggestion of a curl. She looked with disgust at herself until tears blinded her. Then she hurled the comb across the room with all her might and went to the window and cried helplessly. She had been trying for the past ten years to improve the looks of her hair, but each year it became thinner and less manageable and she had to cut it a little shorter from time to time. The ends barely reached to the bottom of her ears by then and she hated to think what she would look like in another ten years.

She did not know how long she had been sitting at the window when she heard Lucy Trotter's high-pitched voice. The house next door was only a few feet away and the two dwellings had been so constructed that the windows faced each other.

'If the rest of the decent people of Agricola had to live next door to you,' Lucy was saying in her piercing voice, 'they wouldn't sleep a wink till they'd run you clear out of Cherokee

19

County. God is certainly punishing the whole sinful town by letting you stay here and torment us like this.'

'I'm not bad,' Molly said. 'Honest, I'm not. I'm just like anybody else. Sometimes I might slip, but I always try to step right back up again when it's all over. Lucy, you've been married so long that you've forgotten what an ordinary woman has to do to get along in the world.'

Lucy was a thin nervous woman of forty with greying hair. She taught the women's Bible class at the Methodist Church on Sundays. The first time Molly attended the class after marrying Putt, Lucy stood up and announced that she would not teach the Bible to the women as long as Molly was present. That almost created a scandal in the church, because all the women wanted to know what Lucy Trotter knew about Molly that they did not already know. Reverend Bigbee had to take charge of the class himself, and after services that morning he took Lucy aside and asked her why she had made such a scene in church. Lucy told him that she would not teach the Bible to Molly as long as she persisted in standing naked at her window and showing off where Clyde could see her. Reverend Bigbee advised Lucy to pull down her own shades and get Clyde interested in crossword puzzles.

'You're raising poor innocent Lily to be just like you,' Lucy was saying. 'You're doing it on purpose too, because sinners like you want company. Lily's going to end up no better than she ought to be, unless she ends up in the state reformatory first. That's where you should have been sent twenty years ago, and we wouldn't have had people like you in our town. I've told Perry never to go anywhere near Lily. I don't want my son contaminated by your kind. I'd die of shame and mortification if he was ever seen with her.'

'I wish you'd stop picking on me, Lucy,' Molly implored. 'I've always tried to do right.'

'The sure hand of God is sending you and Lily both straight to where you belong, and the quicker you get there the better off this town will be. It's a crying shame for respectable people like me to have to live next door to your kind. Why don't you go where you belong?'

'I never did have much of a chance in life, after my folks

died, and it's not my fault if I don't know all the ways there are to be good. I try, though.'

'I'm not interested in your excuses. The devil makes the best excuses of all, and everybody knows how bad he is.'

'But, Lucy, if you'd help me instead of—'

Lucy jerked down the shade over her window. Molly continued to sit where she was while she thought about what Lucy had said and wondered what she could do to make Lucy stop finding fault with her. She knew something was wrong with the way she was raising Lily, but she did not know what to do about it. More than anything else she wanted to keep Lily from having to live the kind of life she had been forced into when her parents died, and she believed the only way Lily could escape it was by marrying at the earliest possible time. She realized that Lily would be better off if she had gone to school longer, but she would soon be seventeen and there was no time for her to stop and go back to school.

She got up and looked at herself in the mirror again. All day she had been worrying about Lily's future and wondering what she was going to do now that Putt was gone. The rent had to be paid some way and she and Lily had to have food and clothes. She had barely enough money in her purse to buy a few more gallons of wine and, when that was gone, she would have to get money somewhere, somehow. Putt had left her nothing, and she still had his funeral expenses to pay. It made her feel more discouraged than ever to think about her plight and she wished she were dead. Shutting her eyes at the sight of herself, she turned away and went to the kitchen for more wine.

Lily had the radio turned on and Molly opened the door and went into her room on her way back from the kitchen. She opened the jug and poured herself another tumblerful, thinking that if she could drink enough of it she could forget her troubles for a while. Lily was stretched out on the bed face downward listening to the music. She had taken off her black lace step-ins and folded them carefully over the back of a chair. The sight of the garment reminded Molly of the one she had made too small for herself, and she quickly snatched it up and put it out of sight in the dresser drawer.

Molly had just sat down again when she heard somebody knock at the front door. Lily immediately sat upright and listened. After a few moments the knocking became louder, and Lily got up and left the room.

She was gone for about ten minutes, during which time Molly drank two more tumblersful of wine, and when she came back, Lily threw herself, laughing, across the bed.

'Who was that, honey?' Molly asked her. 'What are you laughing about so much?'

'It was Perry Trotter,' Lily said. 'He wanted me to go walking with him.'

'What's so funny about that?'

'With Perry Trotter? Mama, he's so young it's pitiful.'

'He's the same age you are, honey,' Molly reminded her. 'Don't forget that.'

They both heard a series of knocks on the front door.

'That's him again,' Lily said. 'He can knock all he wants to. I'm not interested.'

'Maybe he wants to marry you, Lily.'

'You're joking, Mama,' she said, laughing.

'It's no joking matter, honey. The time has come when you've got to stop fooling around and not getting anywhere. A girl's best years is a mighty short stretch in life. You've got to get a man while you can.'

'I'd rather go back to school than marry Perry Trotter,' Lily said.

Perry was knocking louder than ever. Molly turned her head and listened for several moments.

'He's a persistent little cuss,' she said, laughing a little. 'It's a pity he's so young, though. If he was five years older, he'd be worth considering. That's something I want you to start thinking about, Lily. We've got to look out for ourselves from now on, and there's no time to lose. A woman's best years is the shortest stretch in life.'

Molly poured another drink of wine and drank it down in a long noisy gulp.

'I'll bet Lucy Trotter doesn't know Perry's over here,' she said, laughing to herself. 'She'd have a fit if she found out.'

'He pretends to go to bed and then crawls out the window,'

Lily told her. 'He does that every time he wants to get out at night.'

'How do you know so much about it?'

'I went walking with him once. We went over to the Baptist Church and sat on the back steps.'

'You never told me about it before,' Molly said. 'What did you do over there?'

'Nothing, but just sit there. Honest, Mama.'

'I suppose you'd say he didn't even kiss you?'

'He didn't, Mama. You don't know Perry.'

'What's the matter with him? Why didn't he kiss you?'

'That's just the way he is. He didn't even try to hold hands. He just sat there all the time with his hands in his pockets.'

'He must have done something if he took you walking over behind the Baptist Church.'

'He talked.'

'Talked?' Molly said. 'Talked about what?'

'About the high school basketball team.'

Molly had begun to giggle and she had to put the tumbler on the table to keep from spilling the wine. She was soon giggling so loudly that they could no longer hear Perry on the front porch.

'Mama, please stop before it's too late,' Lily begged. She got up and went to her mother, but Molly pushed her away. 'Don't start that again, Mama. You know what it does to you every time. You'll go all to pieces.'

'Go away, Lily!' she yelled, playfully slapping at her. 'Leave me alone now!' she cried, her voice ending in a high-pitched scream.

A moment later she slid from the chair and rolled on the floor. Her giggles had already become convulsive and uncontrollable. Her heavy body struck a chair, upsetting it with a resounding crash. Lily watched her mother helplessly.

'I can see him now—talking about basketball!' she whooped. When she reached the whooping stage of her giggling spells, it was useless to try to stop her. She opened her eyes and looked up at Lily standing above her, and immediately went into another spasm of giggling. Her massive body shook and trembled. 'I wish I could've been there,' she yelled up at Lily. 'That must

23

have been a sight to see—Perry Trotter sitting there on the back steps of the Baptist Church talking about the basketball team! What does he think people go out behind the Baptist Church for at night, anyway!' She began speaking each time in a low precise tone, and then her excited voice gradually rose until she ended in a prolonged whooping scream. 'Sitting on the Baptist steps—talking about basketball! Sitting on the Baptist steps—with his hands in his pockets—and all the time his little dilly so stiff it would've punched a hole in a ginhouse roof.' Her yells and screams were so loud that Lily ran and closed the windows so the neighbours would not hear her. Molly's voice had become hoarse and husky. 'What a life for the female element!' she cried in a piercing scream. 'You wait all night behind the Baptist Church for a man to get up his courage and then find out he's too bashful to use it!' The spasm of giggling had weakened her so much by then that her voice was becoming thin and squeaky. She rolled over two or three times, but she was too weak to keep it up, and so she lay helplessly exhausted on her back while tears streamed from her eyes. 'Oh, my God!' she moaned. 'Put me to bed in a hurry, Lily, and then give me a good full-size dose of vitamins. I don't know when I've needed the shots this bad before.'

Lily went to Molly's room and found the little black case in the dresser drawer. While she was filling the syringe with fluid, Molly came crawling into the room from the hall. Before Lily could help her into bed, Molly fell face downward on the floor. With a weak motion of her hand she motioned for Lily to hurry and give her the injection. Lily plunged the needle deep into Molly's fleshy rump. With a faint cry that was part giggle and part scream, Molly jerkily indicated with a wavering finger that she wanted a second injection.

When Lily finally got her mother into bed, Molly lay quietly with a blissful smile on her puffy round face while the quilts were being tucked in around her. After Lily had turned off the light and was leaving the room, she heard her mother giggle faintly to herself in the darkness.

Chapter 3

MOLLY woke up determined to do something about finding a way to pay the rent and buy food and she sat on the back porch all morning thinking of all possible means of getting money. At one time she had almost made up her mind to sew and give injections, but a small doubt persisted and she decided reluctantly that the income would be too inadequate and unreliable. What she wanted was an assured weekly sum of money that would provide wine and food as well as pay the rent, and by early afternoon she had finally made up her mind to get a job clerking in one of the stores and to work at it until either she or Lily could get married. Elated by her decision, she got dressed right away and left the house.

While she was walking down the shady street to the courthouse square she decided that if she could make fifteen dollars a week she would have no more worries, because that would pay the fifteen dollars a month rent and leave enough over to keep her well. Just before reaching the square, she told herself that if she had a job clerking in a woman's dress shop she could get all the clothes she wanted for both Lily and herself at reduced prices. The prospect of getting a lot of new clothes made her feel exuberantly happy.

She went straight to the Height of Fashion, the larger of the two dress shops in town and asked for the manager. There was only one clerk in the store, and no customers. The manager was a woman Molly had never seen before, and she laughed outright when Molly told her what she wanted. Molly was so angry and provoked that she was on the verge of slapping the woman's face and would have done so if she had not turned and walked away when she did. The clerk tried to interest Molly in a rack of summer dresses that were on special sale, but Molly glared at her threateningly and stalked out of the place.

In the next block was the Mode O'Day, the only other dress shop in town, and Molly, muttering to herself, hurried down the street.

There were several customers in the Mode O'Day when Molly walked in, and Sam Wiggins, the owner, recognized her at once. He came up to her with a jovial smile on his ruddy round face and shook hands with her.

'It's good to see you again, Mrs. Bowser,' he said, stepping back and bowing to her. 'I'm so glad you dropped in. What can we do for you today? We've just unpacked a wonderful shipment of afternoon casuals.'

'What I came in for was to see if you had a job I could have,' she said right away.

The smile vanished from Sam's face.

'Well, no,' he said with a frown while he shook his head, 'I don't think so, Mrs. Bowser. I hire only experienced saleswomen, you know. Besides, this's the slack season in the dress business, and my clerks are working on commission now, anyway. I'm awfully sorry, Mrs. Bowser.'

'I know a lot about dresses,' Molly spoke up hopefully. 'I've always done a lot of needlework.'

'There might be some alteration work later. Right now we're in the middle of the slack—'

'You mean alter dresses to fit?' she said.

Sam nodded doubtfully. He looked as if he were sorry he had ever mentioned alterations.

'Why, that's what I'm best at, Sam,' Molly told him enthusiastically. 'I can do anything with a dress. Mrs. Billings used to say I could take an old tow-sack and make the average woman look like a bride on her honeymoon. Maybe you've noticed how well my daughter Lily's dresses fit her. I'm always doing something to the neckline or something to the hips or something like that for her. Young girls her age just have to have attractive clothes if they're to make an impression on a man.'

26

'I guess that's right,' Sam said uneasily.

'How much do you pay, Sam?' she asked excitedly.

'I couldn't pay enough to make it worth your while, Mrs. Bowser.' He backed away toward the rear of the store. 'I think it'd be better if you tried one of the other stores in town, Mrs. Bowser, I'm sorry.'

Molly followed him to the workroom door.

'All you have to do is give me a trial, Sam. I'll work at piece-work rates. It'll add up.'

Sam went into the workroom and sat down on the edge of a sewing-table. Molly came in and took off her hat.

'Now, just give me a dress to work on, Sam, and I'll show you what I can do,' she told him. 'That'll prove I know how to do good work on women's dresses.'

'Somebody ought to give you some advice, Mrs. Bowser,' he said earnestly. 'Maybe it's not my place, but I knew Putt well, and I'd like to do something to help you. Why don't you leave town and get a job keeping house for somebody out in the county? Nobody in Agricola is going to give you work. Every woman in town remembers when you lived at Mrs. Hawkins' boarding-house and they're afraid to have you around. My wife wouldn't stand for you working here in the store with me all day. She'd make me fire you the minute she found out. Now, why don't you leave before you cause somebody a lot of trouble?'

One of the clerks came to the door and beckoned to Sam. He went out into the aisle where a customer was waiting. He was gone for so long that Molly went out to see what he was doing.

She recognized the customer instantly. Mrs. Sadie Hart, the school principal's wife, was holding up a floral-print silk dress. Mrs. Hart was a large middle-aged woman with heavy calves and large drooping hips.

'Mrs. Hart would like to have this dress let out somewhat, Mr. Wiggins,' the clerk was saying. 'It's the only size we have left in this particular dress.'

Before Sam had an opportunity to say anything, Molly stepped forward and took the measuring tape from the clerk. She put it first around Mrs. Hart's waist and then around her hips. Then she lifted Mrs. Hart's skirt and inspected the seams of the dress she was wearing. Frowning, she dropped the skirt and shook her head.

'You'd better make up your mind that you're going to have to wear forty-fours, Mrs. Hart,' Molly told her. 'If anybody asked me, I'd say you've worn your last forty-two, unless you get busy and reduce. There's no sense in keeping on buying forties and forty-twos and trying to let them out.' She slapped Mrs. Hart familiarly on the hip. 'Your fanny's too big for anything less than a forty-four.'

Mrs. Hart's face turned crimson. Sam glared at Molly.

'Well, what's so funny about that?' Molly asked. 'Just look at me. I've got the biggest fanny in town, and I couldn't even squeeze into a forty-six if I didn't wear a girdle.'

Sam gave Molly a rough push and shoved her into the workroom. He followed her inside and slammed the door.

'You damn fool, you!' he yelled at her angrily. 'Look at what you've gone and done now! Mrs. Hart'll never come back to the Mode O'Day again! She'll do all her buying at the Height of Fashion after this! And she was one of my best customers, too!'

'I was only telling her the truth,' Molly said innocently. 'Somebody ought to tell her she can't get away with trying to wear those forty-two's. If she took off that corset she's wearing, she'd bust the seams of even a forty-four.'

'You damn fool, you! I'm not in business to tell women what size dresses they ought to wear!' Sam shouted. 'I'd go broke in a day's time if I didn't sell them what they wanted.' He sat down on the table and stared unhappily at the floor. 'This's not your type of work, Mrs. Bowser. You'd better go right away before something else dreadful happens.'

Molly burst into tears. She dropped into a chair and sobbed pathetically. Sam took one look at her and began pacing the floor.

'I'm just a poor widow-woman trying to earn a living,' she sobbed. 'I don't know what's going to happen to me now. It looks like as soon as a middle-aged woman's husband dies the whole world starts picking on her. They don't want to help her none at all. I can't help being a poor middle-aged widow-woman.'

'Why don't you go and live with your kinfolks then?' Sam suggested desperately.

'I don't have a single solitary speck of kin, except Lily,' Molly wailed. 'I never did have near kin after my mother and father died and I went to live with the Satterfields. I'm all alone now that Putt's gone. It looks like nobody wants me to keep on living.'

'I hate to see you in such a fix, Mrs. Bowser,' he said nervously. 'If I hear of anybody looking for help, I'll certainly tell them about you.' He went to the door and stood there undecidedly with his hand on the knob. 'Maybe it'd be best if you went on home now, Mrs. Bowser.'

'Would you like to have some vitamins, Sam?' she asked him. 'I can give you a shot for only a dollar. They'll perk you up like nobody's business.'

'No, I don't want no vitamins,' he said impatiently. 'I don't believe in the damn fool things.'

Molly covered her face with her hands and began to sob convulsively again. Sam watched her for a moment and then he took five dollars from his pocket and went over to her. He nudged her until she looked up. As soon as she saw the money, her face brightened and her tears stopped. She grabbed the bill and threw her arms around Sam. She had pushed him back against the wall before he succeeded in loosening her grip. He got away from her and went to the door.

'You'd better go now, Mrs. Bowser,' he said, shaken.

Molly put the money into her purse while he was opening the door.

'That was a mighty nice thing for you to do, Sam,' she said as she went toward him. He could see that she was going to flatten him against the wall again, and he stepped aside just in time. 'If you ever get the feeling that you want to see me for a good time, I'll always be pleased to see you, Sam. I don't say that to everybody, because I'm particular about my company. You know where I live, don't you, Sam?'

Sam nodded and quickly jerked open the door. He pushed her out of the workroom and locked the door on the inside.

Molly walked out of the Mode O'Day and went straight

across the square to the drugstore on the corner. First she paid a dollar and a half for a bottle of perfume, and then she bought a jug of wine, paying two dollars for it. By that time it was getting late, and she hurried from the drugstore and started home.

She passed the taxi stand at the courthouse steps with no more than a casual glance at the cabs and drivers, and she was startled when she heard somebody call her by name. She stopped and looked over her shoulder.

One of the drivers was walking slowly toward her.

'Taxi, Mrs. Bowser?' he said.

'How did you know my name?' she asked, surprised.

'I remember you, Molly,' he said familiarly. 'I'm Joe. I used to drive you once in a while when you lived at Mrs. Hawkins' boarding-house. Remember?'

She walked back to one of the cabs with Joe. He was short and dark with a friendly ingratiating smile. It had been a long time since she had seen him, but all at once he looked familiar. Molly nudged him with her elbow.

'Oh, sure!' she said then. 'I remember you now, Joe. I guess I will ride home for a change. I'm sort of tired out from so much walking.'

Joe opened the cab door and helped her in. She placed the jug on the seat beside her and leaned back comfortably. The taxi circled the courthouse and turned up Muscadine Street. They had gone several blocks when Joe slowed down the cab and looked over his shoulder at her.

'How've you been, Molly?' he asked casually.

'Pretty well,' she told him.

'Keeping yourself busy these days?'

'Oh, I have my busy spells and I have my lazy spells.'

'Don't we all?' he said agreeably.

He drove another block before looking back again.

'I thought maybe you'd left town, Molly.'

'No, I'm still here.'

'What's your phone number out there?'

'I don't have a phone, Joe.'

'That's too bad,' he said, shaking his head.

'I think so myself sometimes,' she agreed.

30

'If I wanted to ring you up, I couldn't, could I?'

'The Trotters next door have a phone,' she said. There was a short pause. 'But Lucy Trotter wouldn't let me use it, anyway.'

'Well, that's not quite the same thing,' Joe said, shaking his head. 'I might be wanting to give you a ring late at night after they'd gone to bed, anyway. That wouldn't be good.'

'That's right,' she said wondering. 'It wouldn't be a good thing to do, late at night.'

'Well, I'll be thinking about it, anyway,' he told her. 'I might think of something.'

'You do that, Joe.'

'I sure will, Molly.'

The cab stopped in front of the house. It was dark by then and Molly knew Lily had not come home, because no lights had been turned on. She felt so lonely that she did not want to leave the taxi. Joe opened the cab door and stood waiting for her to get out.

'Do you want me to take you somewhere else, Molly?' he asked her.

She was silent for a moment. 'I don't have anywhere else to go, Joe,' she told him finally and got out.

She gave him fifty cents from her purse.

'Thanks, Molly,' he said, slamming the cab door. 'When you want a taxi, just phone down to the stand and ask for Joe. If you can't get to a phone, just send word to me and I'll be right along. I'll take care of you. I mind my own business when I make a run, and you never have to worry, because I always keep my mouth shut and know nothing.'

'I'll remember that,' she told him quickly.

'So long, Molly. I'll be seeing you.'

'So long, Joe.'

When she reached the front steps, she heard the taxi drive away. She turned around and watched the red tail-light disappear in the darkness. The moment the lights were out of sight she wanted to call Joe back, but it was too late then.

She felt even more lonely when she opened the door and stepped into the hall. She stood in the darkness of the silent house feeling as though she were the last human being left

31

living on the earth. Crying a little, she turned on the lights and went to the kitchen to open the jug of wine.

She drank the first tumblerful as quickly as she could.

'Mama loves papa,' she said to herself in a husky voice as she gazed at the empty glass in her hand.

After drinking another tumblerful she picked up the jug and carried it to her room. Tossing her hat aside, she took off her clothes. She had to pull and jerk at the tight girdle until she was out of breath, all the time wishing Lily was there to help her. When she finally got it off, she kicked it out of sight under the bed. Her brassiere had split again, and she threw it aside disgustedly.

She stood in front of the mirror, twisting and turning in order to see herself in all positions. In the end, as always, she was thoroughly disgusted by her appearance, and she made an ugly face at herself and stuck out her tongue.

She was still standing in front of the mirror when she heard somebody on the front porch. It was about nine o'clock, and still too early for Lily to come home. She listened to the knocking for several moments before putting on her dressing-gown and leaving the room.

The hall light was still burning when she opened the front door, and she was startled to see Perry Trotter's agitated face before her. Perry was startled by the sight of her, too, and he hastily took several steps backwards, at the same time digging his hands deeper into his pockets.

'What do you want, Perry?' she asked peevishly.

'Is—is—Lily at home, Mrs. Bowser?'

Molly shook her head.

'When will she be home, Mrs. Bowser?'

'I don't know. I suppose she's gone to the movies.'

'She'll be here after that, won't she?'

'What do you want to see Lily about?'

'I just want to see her, Mrs. Bowser,' he said in a pleading voice. 'I just want to. That's all.'

'Why don't you stop bothering Lily? She's got other things to think about.'

'I like Lily, Mrs. Bowser.'

'That's no reason, if that's all you can say. There're plenty of other girls in town your age. Go see some of them.'

'Lily's the only one I like, Mrs. Bowser. That's why I want to see her.'

'Well, you can stop wasting your time, Perry. Lily's thinking about getting married, and you're too young for that.'

'I sure would like to marry her, Mrs. Bowser,' he said earnestly. He dug his hands deeper and deeper into his pockets. 'I sure would like to do that, Mrs. Bowser.'

'Well, you can't,' she told him flatly. 'You're not old enough, for one thing. You couldn't even support yourself, if you had to, much less both of you.' She stopped and laughed at Perry. 'When Lily marries, she's going to marry a man who can give her everything.'

'Who is he?' Perry asked, distressed.

'I don't know yet,' she said, 'but it won't be you, Perry, so you'd better save yourself a lot of worry and shoe leather and forget about wanting to marry Lily.'

Perry stood at the edge of the porch looking forlorn and dejected.

'You'd better go on home before your mama finds out where you've been,' she told him. 'You know what she'd do to you if she ever caught you over here.'

She closed the door with a determined slam and went back to her room. She did not hear him again after that.

After getting into bed Molly poured herself some more wine. Then she lay back, propping her head and shoulders against the pillows, and began drinking the wine with careless noisy sips, giggling a little each time some of it dripped from the corners of her mouth and trickled down her bare skin.

It was after midnight when Molly was awakened by the sound of somebody walking down the hall. She opened her eyes just as Lily came into the room.

'What's the matter, Mama?' she asked, her eyes blinking in the strong light. 'Why are you up so late?'

'Where've you been?' Molly demanded roughly. 'Did you go to the movies?'

'I've already seen that picture. They won't have a new one till Saturday.'

'Then where were you?'

'On a date.'

Molly sat upright. 'Who was he, honey?' she asked expectantly. 'Is he nice? Did he ask you for another date?'

'Oh, it was just somebody,' she said with a shrug.

'What's his name?'

Lily looked down at the floor, avoiding her mother's piercing eyes.

'Doc Logan.'

'Doc Logan!' Molly said angrily. Her arm struck the empty wine glass and it crashed to pieces on the floor. 'What's got into you, Lily? I've told you before to stay away from him! Doc can do you more harm, and do it quicker, than any man in town. First thing you know nobody can do anything with you, after you've been with him enough times. He can ruin you faster than a rock can slide off a ginhouse roof. It'd be all right if you were marrying a doctor, but you can be sure it won't be Doc Logan. He's got a wife and he's nearly fifty years old. He's not going to marry you or any of those girls he gets down there in his office. Now, you stop having dates with Doc before you're ruined for an ordinary man. I know what goes on down there in that office of his at night. Now, you stay away from doctors after this, specially Doc Logan. Do you hear me?'

'But he's so nice, Mama,' Lily protested. 'I just go wild about him. Everything is so wonderful——'

'I don't want to hear any more,' Molly said sharply. 'I know all about it. I'm going to get busy right away and find somebody to marry you before it's too late. I thought I could trust you to go out and find a man your own self, but now I see I've got to do it for you.'

Chapter 4

MOLLY and Lily were in the kitchen eating breakfast when they first heard somebody on the front porch, but there had been no knock at the door and Molly thought some of the neighbours' children were playing hide-and-go-seek around the house. They were drinking coffee and eating hot dogs again. The hot dogs had first been rolled in mustard, then in biscuit dough, and baked in a deep bread pan in the oven. Breakfast was Molly's favourite meal, and hot dogs were her favourite dish, and she often ate as many as seven or eight of them at a sitting, liberally spreading an additional helping of mustard on each bite of hot dog.

They had eaten the last hot dog and were still sitting at the kitchen table drinking coffee when they heard footsteps in the hall. Lily and Molly looked inquiringly at each other. This time the footsteps were heavy and deliberate.

'You'd better go see who that is, honey,' Molly said, nodding toward the hall.

Lily went as far as the door and stopped. A strange man dressed in overalls was walking towards the kitchen. Lily ran back into the kitchen and stood behind the table.

'What's the matter, honey? Who's out there?'

Lily pointed at the door. Molly turned around slowly.

'Howdy,' he said casually, as though he had known them all his life. Molly, her mouth falling open, thought she had seen him somewhere before, because his face looked familiar. He was a medium-size man of about forty with a heavy shock of uncombed black hair. In addition to his faded overalls he was wearing a pair of heavy work shoes and a tan cotton jacket several sizes too small for him. A snaggle-toothed smile appeared on his unshaven face. 'Well, howdy, folks,' he said ingratiatingly.

'What do you want?' Molly asked, unmoved by his grinning face.

'Ain't you Molly?' he said.

She nodded slowly, still wondering why he looked like somebody she had seen before.

'Well, I'm Jethro,' he told her, nodding his head as he looked at Lily and back again at Molly.

'Jethro who?'

'Jethro—Putt's brother.'

Molly caught her breath. 'Putt's brother?'

'Didn't Putt ever tell you about me?'

'Putt said he had a brother, but he thought he was dead, because he hadn't heard from him in eight or ten years.'

'That's me,' Jethro stated proudly. 'I didn't have no cause to write him a letter.'

'You do look a lot like him,' she agreed.

'We always did have a family resemblance.'

Molly got up and put the coffee pot back on the stove to heat, at the same time taking a good look at Jethro while he was facing Lily. The corners of her mouth turned up scornfully when she saw the droopy hang of his slack-seated overalls. After that she got a cup and saucer from the cupboard and placed them on the table. Jethro immediately drew up a chair and sat down. Leaning back, he regarded Lily with an appraising stare.

'You ain't Putt's girl?' he said to her, shaking his head.

Lily shook her head.

'Then whose girl is you?' he asked, glancing inquiringly at Molly.

'She's my daughter, Lily,' Molly said. 'By a previous——'

Jethro nodded with a satisfied look on his face and stared at Lily some more. She quickly sat down.

'She's a fine-looking one, all right,' he commented. 'How old is she?'

'Sixteen,' Molly told him.

Jethro grinned broadly.

'I've seen a heap worse,' he said.

Molly poured coffee into his cup and then refilled Lily's and her own. Jethro tipped the cup and filled the saucer, setting the cup on the oilcloth. Then he lifted the saucer with both hands and, with elbows resting on the table, noisily sucked and sipped at the puddle of hot black coffee. Molly sat down, regarding him with a suspicious frown.

'What do you want here?' she asked pointedly. 'What did you come for? It's too late for the funeral. Putt was buried last Wednesday.'

'He was?' Jethro said with apparent surprise. 'I didn't know they'd box him up and put him out of the way that quick. I only heard about it yesterday morning, but it took me all this time to get here. I was working for a farmer over in Woodbine County and I had to quit and draw down my pay before I could get started.'

'That's too bad,' Molly said. 'I know you'd have enjoyed the funeral. It was real pretty.'

'I never was much for going to funerals,' he said with a shake of his head. 'Somebody always gets left behind, and that always makes me feel sad.'

No one said anything for a while. Jethro filled the saucer again and sucked at the coffee. From time to time he looked over the rim of the saucer at Lily, but she averted her eyes each time she found herself being stared at.

'Well,' Molly said finally, 'I guess you'll be going back, now that the funeral's over.'

Jethro promptly shook his head and put down the saucer.

'No,' he told her, 'I don't aim to. I'm going to be kept pretty busy for a while looking after Putt's estate.'

'Putt didn't leave a solitary thing,' she spoke up.

'He was bound to leave something behind. A man always collects some odds and ends in a lifetime. I was talking to some folks downtown this morning, and they said he owned a little push cart, for one thing. After I've looked around a while I'll locate the odds and ends. It'll all add up to make it worthwhile. He must have left an extra pair of shoes behind, and things like that. It's my duty to look after things like that for Putt. He'd want me to.'

'Everything he left belongs to me,' Molly told him in a sharp tone of warning. 'I'm his widow under the law.'

'Well, now, let's not get fidgety about it, Molly. I didn't come all the way over here to take what rightfully belongs to you. It'll all work out fair and square in the end. We'll do some swapping and trading to make things come out even. Why, I'll probably turn up things you didn't know nothing at all about, and in that way there'll be more to go round. Now, I could use a few shirts and some socks right away——'

'No you don't!' she said coldly. 'Everything in this house is mine.'

Jethro leaned back and pushed his hand into his overalls pocket. When he withdrew his hand, he was fingering a thick roll of greenbacks.

'I drew down my pay that was coming to me when I left Woodbine County, and I don't aim to be a burden on nobody. I want to pay my share. I always said that was the fair and square thing to do.'

Molly's hostile expression suddenly became warm and friendly. Her eyes twinkled as a smile spread over her face.

'Lily, get your Uncle Jethro some more hot coffee,' she said graciously. 'Fill up his cup for him.' While Lily was getting the coffee, Molly leaned forward, moving her chair closer to Jethro, and rested her arms and heavy breasts on the table. Jethro uttered a pleased grunt as he observed her intimate gesture. 'I'm awfully easy to get along with, Jethro,' she told him, partly closing her eyes. 'I hope you didn't get the wrong impression about me. I've been a little upset the past few days, but that's not my real nature. Everybody who's ever known me will tell you I have a nice loving disposition.'

Jethro, grinning, moved his chair closer.

'Now, you just make yourself at home, Jethro,' she went on hurriedly. 'I want you to feel that this's as much your home as it is mine. If there's anything you need, like some of Putt's shirts and things, don't hesitate to speak of it. You'll want some darning and mending done. If there's something special you like to eat, like hog sausage and yams, just let me know. I'm not a bad cook when I set myself to it, I was always pretty

38

much of a homebody, too, and there's nothing I like better than doing things for a man around the house.'

Jethro was nodding and watching Lily from the corners of his eyes while Molly was talking. When she finished, there was a period of silence in the kitchen, and Molly reached over and nudged Jethro with her elbow. Startled, he jerked himself up instantly.

'That's the truth,' he said a moment later, looking confused. Molly said nothing more, and presently he pushed back his chair and stretched his long thin arms over his head. 'Well, I reckon I'll take a look around,' he said, getting up. He went to the door leading to the back porch and looked critically at the yard. He stood there for several minutes inspecting it with deep interest. 'I'll step outside in the back,' he said as he started out. 'I always did like to look at folks' backyards. You can tell more about folks by looking at their trash piles in the backyard than you can any other way.'

Molly followed him as far as the porch steps. She stood and watched while Jethro walked out to the big trash pile and poked into it with a stick. He dug out a few tin cans, an old shoe, and a rusty bicycle chain. Putt had always brought a lot of odds and ends home while he was alive and most of the things he picked up on the streets and elsewhere around town were sooner or later thrown into the back yard. Whenever Molly found something broken or useless in the house that she wanted to get rid of, she carried it to the back porch and slung it into the yard. Every once in a while she gave a small coloured boy a nickel or a dime to rake up the trash and litter into a pile. After all that time the accumulation of tin cans, rusty wheels, and other discarded matter had built up one pile that was about waist high and several smaller ones that were constantly increasing in size.

Lucy Trotter had seen Jethro from her kitchen window, and she walked out on her back porch and looked at him curiously as he bent over the big trash pile. She did not say anything until he turned around, enabling her to get a good look at his face.

'It's the punishment of God,' she said in a loud hysterical voice that could be heard to the end of the block. 'It's another

Bowser come to torment our souls. I don't know what the good people of this town have done to have this kind of punishment inflicted upon us. God have mercy on us!'

Jethro had turned from the trash pile and gone to the fence. With mouth agape, he watched Lucy until she had finished talking, and then he swung a leg over the low pickets. Lucy screamed and ran into the house, slamming and locking the door. Jethro put his other leg over the fence, strolled over to the Trotters' trash pile and calmly began poking into it with his stick. Finding nothing that interested him after carefully looking through the accumulation, he swung first one leg and then the other over the picket fence and came back to the porch where Molly had been waiting.

'Those folks over there in the house next door sure must be pretty poor and puny,' he commented with a deprecating shake of his head. 'You ought to see their trash pile, Molly. I couldn't find nothing of account but some old broken bottles and a few tin cans. Putt left a fine trash pile out here. I'm going back out there in a day or two and look through it some more. It's a jim-dandy.'

Molly smiled, glad to hear him speak the way he did about Lucy Trotter.

'She's an old fool,' Molly said, going to the door and waiting for Jethro to follow her. 'All she lives for is to make trouble.' They were walking down the hall, and when Molly reached the door to her room, she smiled at Jethro and stepped inside. Jethro came in, craning his neck and looking curiously at the disarray of clothing and quilts on the floor and chairs. Molly immediately began gathering up the things nearest at hand and tossing them into the closet. 'Lucy Trotter's husband is a fine man,' she continued. 'His name's Clyde, and he owns a planing mill out on the edge of town. But she's not good for anything. All Lucy Trotter lives for is to make trouble.'

Jethro selected a chair that had been cleared of dresses and quilts and sat down. Molly kicked a pair of shoes under the bed.

'I always did like to keep things nice and orderly,' she said, looking around for something else to do. 'I guess it's just my nature to be so particular.' She rearranged the comb and brush

40

on her dresser and swept a pile of rubber and wire curlers into a drawer. Then with a sigh of satisfaction she sat down on the bed. 'I just happened to think that we're all out of a few things in the kitchen today, Jethro,' she said earnestly. 'Now, if it's not too much bother, Jethro, when you go downtown, you can bring back some lard and flour, and a few little things like a couple of pounds of hot dogs and some canned beans. While you're about it, you can get a jug of wine, too. I always like to keep a gallon or so on hand, and I don't have much left in the house right now. It's a lot cheaper to buy it by the gallon, and make sure you get red wine instead of the other.'

They both could hear Lily in the next room, and Jethro cocked his head to one side and listened interestedly.

'She's a mighty fine-looking young girl,' he said. 'It's been a long time since I've laid eyes on one that pert.'

'Who, Lily?' Molly said, annoyed. 'Oh, she's just a child, Jethro, and it'll be a long time yet before she grows up. She's not like us grown-ups. All she's interested in are little childish things.' She stopped and watched Jethro anxiously. 'Sometimes I think nobody ever had a more unselfish daughter than Lily is. Do you know what she said to me this morning, Jethro?'

'What?'

'She said she wanted me to have a new pair of shoes, because the ones I've got are too shabby to wear in public.'

Jethro bent over and looked down at Molly's shoes. She was wearing a pair of scuffed brown oxfords which she kept for house wear. Slits had been cut along the outside just above the soles in order to keep her corns and bunions from hurting.

'Those look mighty comfortable to me,' Jethro commented. 'I don't see how you could find another pair that look so easy on the feet.'

'But I'd be ashamed to wear these out on the street where everybody could see me.'

'No, I guess you wouldn't want to do that,' he agreed reluctantly.

'I sure would be proud of a new pair, Jethro. I think I could make ten dollars stretch.'

Jethro looked down at her shoes again, and then he got up and took the roll of money from his pocket. Molly stood up, and he backed part way across the room, at the same time quickly taking ten dollars from the roll. By the time he could get the roll back into his pocket Molly was almost beside him.

'You ought to get Lily a new pair of shoes, too,' he said as he handed her the money. 'It'd be foolish to spend all that on just one pair.'

With a quick motion of her hand, Molly snatched the money from him and wadded it in her palm. Then she threw her arms around him.

'Aw, that's all right, Molly,' he said excitedly. 'I'm glad to do a little thing like that for Lily.'

'I don't know what we'd've done if you hadn't come along, Jethro,' she told him gratefully. He found himself being pushed backward by Molly's powerful body, and a moment later he was pinned helplessly between her and the wall. He was able to get his breath only in short quick gasps as her weight pressed against his chest. He made a desperate effort to push her away, but the crunching weight of Molly's body was more than he could overcome. 'I want you to know how much I appreciate it, Jethro,' she breathed hoarsely in his ear.

He still had not been able to say anything and he was so short of breath that all at once he became limp and completely helpless. Molly sensed something was wrong when his knees gave way. Just when he thought he would never breathe again, she moved back. He sagged forward and she caught him in her powerful arms just before he would have fallen on the floor.

'Jethro, you're weak and all tired out after that long trip from Woodbine County,' she said sympathetically. With his feet dragging on the floor, she carried him to the bed and stretched him upon it. 'I didn't realize how tired you must be,' she said with concern. 'You need vitamins bad.' Jethro's chest was heaving and he was groaning between breaths. He still felt dizzy and he had no idea what Molly was doing when she went to the dresser drawer and took out the small leatherette case. 'Now, this is going to make you feel like a new all-around man, Jethro,' she was saying to him.

Molly slipped the overall straps from his shoulders and turned him over. He still did not know what was happening when he felt his overalls slide down to his knees. There was a quick jab

42

of the needle, and Jethro yelled at the top of his voice. When he tried to move, he found that Molly was sitting astride his back.

'Let me go!' he yelled as loudly as he could, at the same time attempting to dislodge Molly by hitting at her with his elbows. 'You're murdering me! Let me go—let me go!'

'Be quiet, Jethro,' she said calmly. 'This's good for you and you don't know it.'

She pressed the plunger down into the syringe until the injection had been completed. Then she pulled out the needle. Jethro yelled again.

'Now, it's all done and finished,' she said in a kindly voice. 'It's nothing to be afraid of, Jethro.'

'What did you do to me?' he shouted.

Molly got up and sat down on the bed beside him. He watched with trembling hands while she was putting the syringe back into the case.

'I gave you a vitamin shot, Jethro,' she said, smiling down at him. 'That's all it was. Lily and I give each other shots all the time. Now, before you know it you'll be feeling like a new all-around man. You were all wore out and didn't know it.'

Jethro raised his head and saw Lily standing in the doorway.

'What was the matter, Mama?' she asked.

'Oh, nothing, honey,' Molly said calmly. 'I was just giving your Uncle Jethro a shot, and he wasn't used to it. The next time we'll all take shots together, and then he'll see how easy it is.' She gave Jethro a light pat. 'There's nothing to be afraid of, now is there, Jethro? Don't you feel like a new all-around man already?'

He nodded with an eager motion.

'I think maybe I do, sure enough,' he said while a broad grin spread over his face. 'I'm glad I came over here now.' His snaggled teeth gleamed in his mouth. 'You know, I could've lived and died over there in Woodbine County and never known a thing about what went on in the big outside world.'

43

Chapter 5

CHRISTINE BIGBEE sent Mamie, her Negro maid, to ask Molly to come to see her that afternoon if she possibly could, and Molly began getting ready right away. She knew without asking Mamie that Reverend Bigbee had gone out of town, because otherwise Christine would never have dared to send for her, and she told Mamie she would be there within an hour. Molly was always glad when Christine sent for her, because she felt that Christine was the only friend she had in town and, for that matter, the only friend she had ever had anywhere.

Molly's father had been a tenant farmer who worked a crop for Tom Satterfield in the lower end of Cherokee County until she was twelve years old. She had just passed her twelfth birthday when he and her mother were killed by a team of runaway mules that threw all three of them out of the wagon. Her father's head struck a pine tree and he died instantly. Her mother was crushed by the overturned wagon-bed and lived for only a few hours. Molly was badly frightened and one leg was broken, but the Satterfields carried her to their house and took care of her until she was well enough to get up and help with the work. She had no close relatives and Mrs. Satterfield said she could stay there and learn to do household tasks. In the beginning she washed dishes and made beds, but as she grew older and stronger she was given more to do and after two years she was doing all of the household work.

She had been able to go to school for only a few months each year while her parents were alive, usually from December to March, because during the remainder of the time she had to help her mother and father in the fields in the spring and pick cotton

44

in the fall. After going to live with the Satterfields she had no other opportunity to go to school. She remembered hearing her father say many times that he wished she could have the education he and her mother did not have. He had told her many things that made little impression upon her at the time but which she often recalled while she was living with the Satterfields.

She had never forgotten something her father said to her one hot summer afternoon while they were sitting in the shade and resting for a few minutes between rows.

'They didn't make the world for folks like us, Molly,' he told her when she asked for a new pair of shoes to wear to church on Sundays, 'and sometimes I get to thinking and wonder how we came to be here and for what reason. It's a fine place for some folks to be, but there've been a lot of times in my life when I'd rather be dead than have to live like I do. There's a lot like us in the world, too, and most of us are just plain lucky if we manage to stay alive. There'll always be a handful who'll have all the shoes they want, and everything else that goes with them, but folks like us have to work, if we can find the jobs, and still go without new shoes, because somehow we just can't seem to make enough from one year to the next to get all we need. The Satterfields over there will always have all they want, or if they don't then somebody else like them will, because they've got the land and the stock. Folks like us just have to be content with the little that's left over, and there's never much of that after folks like the Satterfields take all they want.'

Molly could not keep from crying when she realized that what he was saying was that she could not have the shoes.

'You'll have to learn to live in want, Molly,' he told her kindly. 'That's the way we were born. After all these years of trying, I'm thankful now just to have enough to keep me alive. There's nothing else for me to live for now, and I won't regret when the time comes to go.'

After Molly had gone to live with the Satterfields and had begun doing their work for them, she was able to understand why her father had been so bitter and discouraged. The Satterfields were not satisfied to have her do only the dish-washing and cooking and bed-making, but whenever they found her resting, they gave her another task to do. She was so tired from one day to the

45

next that she lost the spirit to complain about the work that was forced upon her. They made her get up at five o'clock and milk the cows. After that she cooked breakfast, washed the dishes, cleaned house, churned, cooked dinner, mended, washed the clothes, prepared supper, and washed the dishes again. She was never able to finish her work before nine o'clock at night.

'You're the most ungrateful creature I've ever laid eyes on,' Mrs. Satterfield told her one day when she failed to churn the butter. 'We took you in when you had no place to go, and now you won't do half the things you're supposed to. I've got a good mind to get the strap and beat some appreciation into your lazy good-for-nothing body.'

At first Molly had cried herself to sleep at night, and it always seemed to her that she would no more than close her eyes before one of the Satterfields was pounding on the door and telling her to hurry and get breakfast started. Once she was so tired and sleepy that she fell across the bed while she was dressing, and the next thing she knew Mrs. Satterfield was beating her on the back and shoulders with the heavy leather strap.

When she was fifteen, one of the Satterfield boys, Ed, climbed through her window one night and got into bed with her. She was frightened, but she wanted company and companionship more than anything else in the world, and she cried the rest of the night with happiness. Ed later told his brother, Johnny, and after that one of them came to see her several times a week. After a year she became so fond of Ed and Johnny that she waited hopefully for one of them every night.

Tom Satterfield had always been gruff with her and he rarely said anything unless it was to scold her for something she had failed to do, and she was too surprised to say anything when he climbed through the window one night when both boys were away from home. She was so frightened that the only thing she could remember his saying was that he was going to beat her with the strap if she ever told anybody.

Molly was eighteen when one morning she felt so ill she could not get out of bed, and Mrs. Satterfield got the leather strap and hit her with it until she could not remember anything that happened afterwards. That afternoon Mrs. Satterfield took her to town to see a doctor. When Mrs. Satterfield heard that she was

46

going to have a baby, she threatened to have her arrested or sent to the county home, but the doctor talked to her for a long time, and she finally agreed to let Molly go to the hospital.

They took her home after two weeks and Mrs. Satterfield threatened to beat her and the baby if she ever told anybody who the father was. Molly was not certain herself, because she had slept with both Ed and Johnny, as well as with Tom Satterfield, but she told Mrs. Satterfield that the baby's father was a stranger who came to the house one day while everybody else was away. Mrs. Satterfield did not believe her and made her nail her window down and told her to keep it closed.

Both Ed and Johnny married and moved away shortly after Lily was born. Tom Satterfield found a way to get into her room by removing the sash and he continued coming to her room until George May came there to live. George was a hired man Tom Satterfield engaged to do the work Ed and Johnny formerly had done on the farm. George was about thirty years old then, and Molly was twenty-five, and Tom warned George to stay away from her the first day he was there. A few nights later Molly went down to the barn where George had been given a cot in the harness room. She found George sitting on his cot and playing a harmonica. She went into the harness room and closed the door.

'He told me he'd make trouble for me,' George said fearfully. 'You'd better go away.'

Molly sat down on the cot beside him.

'Don't be scared of him,' she said.

They sat there for an hour while George played the harmonica for her. Then the sudden creaking of the harness room door startled them both. George sprang to his feet. Tom Satterfield came forward, swinging an axe. The blade struck George on the side of the head, the blow glancing downward into his neck. Molly, screaming with fright, ran past Tom before he could catch her and got the door open. She went to the house and got Lily and ran with her out into the field. After running until she fell exhausted, she and Lily huddled in a thicket all night. The next morning she and Lily ran across the field until they reached the road. They walked all morning and that afternoon a man in a logging truck gave them a ride.

It was late in the afternoon when they came to Slowdown, a

47

small crossroads settlement. Most of the dwellings were clustered around a small lunch room and filling station called Roy's Lunch. When Molly first went inside, she could see no one, but when she went up to the counter, a tall unshaven man got up from a stool. The floor was littered with stale bread crusts and flies were clustered on the uncovered sugar bowls.

'We're hungry,' Molly said desperately. 'My little girl hasn't eaten since yesterday.'

'Have you got money?' Roy asked indifferently.

Molly told him she had no money.

'How do you expect to eat if you ain't got money?'

'I'll work for it,' she said pleadingly. 'I'm good at cooking and cleaning. I'll do anything if you'll only give me and my little girl something to eat.'

Roy jerked his thumb in the direction of the kitchen behind him. 'Go get yourself and the little girl something to eat then,' he told her.

Molly made coffee and cooked several slices of ham and some potatoes. As soon as the meal was ready, she and Lily sat down and ate everything she had prepared. After they had finished and washed the dishes, Roy came to the door.

'If you want to clean up around here in the morning, you can stay,' he told her.

Molly was so grateful that she was afraid to say anything, but she nodded her head eagerly. Roy pointed at a door in the rear of the kitchen.

'You can sleep in there,' he said.

There was a large double bed, a dresser with a cracked oval mirror, and a chair in the room. A frayed green roller shade covered the single window. The floor was bare and in need of a thorough cleaning.

Sometime during the night Roy got into her bed, and when she woke up the next morning, it was the first time since she could remember that she did not feel afraid. Roy told her that his wife had died and that she could stay if she wanted to. She thought she ought to tell him about George May, but she decided it would be better if she never told him she had lived at Satterfield farm.

The following summer another girl came to the lunch room

and asked Roy for a job, offering to work for nothing if he would let her stay. She was about eighteen or twenty, and much better looking than Molly, and Roy sent Molly and Lily to the Billings' farm two miles away. Mrs. Billings had been looking for a house-keeper for a month, and she hired Molly immediately. During the time she lived there Mrs. Billings taught her how to do embroidery and all the other fancy needlework she knew. When Lily was fourteen and had just finished her first year in high school, one of the farm hands got into bed with Lily one night, and Molly was so angry when she found him that she got Mr. Billings' shotgun and tried to kill him. He jumped out the win-dow before she could shoot him, though, and the next morning she packed their belongings and took Lily to Agricola, where they rented a room at Mrs. Hawkins' boarding-house. They lived there for a little more than a year before she married Putt Bowser, and it was during that time that she became acquainted with Christine and went to visit her almost every time Reverend Bigbee went out of town for a day or two.

Christine met Molly at the door and took her into the parlour. The house was cool and comfortable and Molly settled herself in a chair and fanned her face briskly. She had hurried through the afternoon heat and beads of perspiration had broken out on her face and neck.

'Well,' she said, taking a deep breath, 'here I am, Christine.'

'You didn't forget to bring the you-know-what, did you, Molly?' she said, smiling as she looked at the small black case in Molly's lap. 'It's been almost a month since you were here the last time.' She got up and closed the door. 'Mamie's awfully curious,' she explained. 'I think she knows too much.'

Christine was a small dark-haired woman of thirty-five, and several years younger than Reverend Bigbee. They had been married for ten years, and before her marriage she had taught school for three years. After they had been married for a few months she found out that the reason for his asking her was because he felt that a married pastor would have more dignity than an unmarried one. Year after year she had tried every means she could think of to win his love and affection, but as time went on he became more austere and less approachable. She was still youthful looking and attractive, and the older church women continued their relentless criticism of her for looking too young and gay to be a minister's wife. If she went to church on Sunday morning with a bright shade of lipstick on, some of the older women were certain to speak to Reverend Bigbee about it after service, and if they disapproved of the depth of her neckline or the length of her skirt, they lost no time in calling it to Reverend Bigbee's attention. He invariably spoke sternly to her afterwards and ordered her to conduct herself in the manner demanded by the congregation. She had come to realize that there was little she could do without having the church women and her husband disapprove. When she taught school, she had always gone to movies every week-end, but Reverend Bigbee disapproved of the movies. She knew better than to attempt to smoke a cigarette in her husband's presence, and the only opportunity she had to smoke was when he was away from the house or out of town.

'Has he gone away?' Molly asked significantly.

'Yes, thank God!' Christine said with a sigh of relief. She had taken a cigarette from a pack and was lighting it defiantly. 'He won't be back till tomorrow.' She puffed a cloud of smoke all around her. 'I'm going to smoke like a God damn furnace, God damn it!'

'I don't know what it'd be like, living with a man who wouldn't let you smoke and do things you wanted,' Molly said. 'But he's bound to like some things, Christine.'

'What things?' she said with a short laugh. 'I wish you'd name just one, Molly. You don't know what hell it is, living with somebody so God damn goody-goody.'

'Well, I could name one or two things he ought to like,' Molly told her.

'You'd be surprised, Molly.' She shook her head sadly. 'Do you know what he does now?'

'What?'

'He reads the Bible aloud in bed every night, that's what. Last night it was the fifth chapter of Luke. I'm a Christian woman, Molly, but there're times when I don't want to hear the Bible read.'

'I don't blame you, Christine. I don't think I could ever get used to that, no matter how religious I wanted to be.'

'One of these days something's going to give, somewhere.

50

It can't keep on like this. It's driving me crazy. The only thing that's helped so far is to swear all over the place when he's away, but that's only temporary. I'll have to do something else. He won't even let me undress without turning out the lights, and I have to wear long-sleeved nightgowns that drag the floor. This morning as soon as he left I took off all my clothes and ran out into the back yard and said "God damn it to hell!" as loud as I could. Of course, Mamie almost died laughing at me. I guess it was a silly thing to do, but I had to do something.'

'I thought I had a troublesome time,' Molly said, 'but I reckon I didn't know how well off I was. I don't know what I'd do if I had to put up with the things you do, Christine.'

Christine lit a fresh cigarette and got up.

'Let's go take some shots, Molly,' she said, opening the door.

Molly followed her down the hall, and when they were in the bedroom, Christine pulled down all the shades and undressed. Molly filled the syringe and sat down on the bed.

'I don't know what I'd do if I couldn't have these once in a while,' Christine told her. 'Please don't ever go away and not come back. You've just got to stay.'

'I'm here to stay,' Molly assured her. 'I'll always be somewhere in town.'

Christine lay face downward across the bed and puffed a cloud of smoke over her head. She suddenly shook with laughter. 'Wouldn't it be funny if Charles walked in now and saw us, Molly?' she asked. 'Wouldn't that be a sight to see?' Molly squeezed her flesh between thumb and forefinger and jabbed the needle into her. 'What do you think he'd do if we tried to give him an injection, Molly? Wouldn't that be something?'

Molly withdrew the needle. 'Do you want another one right away, Christine?' she asked.

'Oh God, yes!' she cried. 'Dozens of them, Molly!'

Molly gave her a second shot and then refilled the syringe again.

'Now, give me one, Christine,' she said, handing Christine the syringe. She took off her dress and lay across the bed. 'We'll want to feel good together,' she said with her face

51

pressed against the spread. 'I don't need the shots as much as you do, but there're plenty for us both.'

When Christine finished injecting the fluid into her, she handed Molly the syringe and quickly lit another cigarette. After that they lay on the bed and smoked one cigarette after another and talked about Reverend Bigbee and his peculiarities.

Chapter 6

LILY had undressed for bed and was listening to dance music on the radio when she heard somebody call to her through the open window. It was between nine and ten o'clock and Molly was still at Christine Bigbee's. Jethro had gone downtown late that afternoon, and Lily could not think of anyone who would be standing outside her window and calling her at that time of night. The moon was shining brightly and, when she raised her head and looked, she could see the top of somebody's head almost on a level with the windowsill. She shut off the radio and waited. After several moments she became curious to know who was there and so she got up and went to the window.

'Hello, Lily,' Perry Trotter said in a frightened voice that was barely a whisper.

'What do you want, Perry?' she said coolly. 'What are you doing out there?'

'I want to see you, Lily,' he said hopefully. He stood on his toes and put both hands on the sill. Lily stepped backward out of the moonlight into the shadow of the room. 'Gee, Lily!' he said eagerly, and a moment later he tried to hoist himself through the window.

'You get away from here, Perry Trotter,' she said, hitting his fingers and the back of his hands with her knuckles.

Perry held on as long as he could, and when Lily gave him a push, he lost his grip on the sill and dropped to the ground.

'Please let me come in, Lily,' he pleaded.

'I can't.'

'Why not? Don't you like me at all, Lily? Why don't you let me come to see you? I like you an awful lot, Lily. Honest, I do! I'm just crazy about you.'

'I can't be bothered with you, Perry Trotter,' she told him ruthlessly. 'Now, go on away. You're too young to interest me.'

'I'm sixteen, Lily,' he said, his hands gripping the sill again. 'That's old enough, isn't it? I've grown up a lot since that night we went over behind the Baptist Church.' He waited, but Lily made no reply. 'How much older would I have to be before you liked me, Lily?'

'Dozens of years,' she said. 'But even then I probably wouldn't like you, Perry.'

'Why not, Lily?'

'Just because, that's why.'

'Even if I liked you more than anybody else in the whole world?'

'That wouldn't make any difference to me.'

'Gee whiz, Lily, I think you're wonderful. I'll always like you. I'll like you as long as I live. I'll never like anybody else, Lily.'

'That doesn't interest me in the least, Perry Trotter. I've got other things to think about. I can't waste my time on you.'

'Do you like somebody else better than you do me?'

'Dozens,' she told him. 'Now, go on away, Perry.'

Perry stood motionlessly for several moments while he gazed longingly at Lily in the moonlight. Then with a swift lurch of his body he swung his right leg over the windowsill and, before Lily could stop him, climbed into the room. At first Lily tried to push him through the window, but Perry was determined, and she was unable to make him leave. Then she ran across the room, but Perry caught her in his arms and held her so tightly that she was helpless. She beat against his chest with her hands, but Perry did not mind that. He put both arms around her and pressed his lips against hers until she finally stopped struggling. Perry began to tremble with excitement after that and his knees felt weak and shaky. It was the first time he had ever kissed her and held her in his arms and he had to sit down on the bed in order to keep his knees from buckling under him. He could feel Lily's body tremble in his arms and he held her more tightly.

'You'll let me stay now, won't you, Lily?' he said hoarsely. 'You won't make me go, will you, Lily?'

Lily did not answer, but her body shook more violently. He pressed his face against hers, moving his lips over her cheeks until he found her mouth. She still did not resist him and she allowed his lips to cling to hers. After a while she was no longer trembling.

'You like me just a little bit, don't you, Lily?' he asked her in a voice that sounded far away. 'I like you so much I don't know how to tell you. Honest, I do, Lily. I'll always like you as long as I live. I'll never like anybody else, Lily.'

He felt her move closer to him and he kissed her for a long time.

'Let's go away and get married, Lily,' he said in a tremulous voice. 'Will you, Lily? Let's go right away before something happens. If we wait, a lot of things are liable to happen. I don't know what, but something might. Let's get married now, Lily. Will you, Lily? Will you do that?'

She pressed her face against his but said nothing.

'We'll go where nobody can find us and make us come back. I'll get a job and make enough money to give you everything you want, Lily. I'll never stop as long as I live. Will you do that, Lily? Please, Lily!'

'I don't want to get married yet,' she said in a low voice. 'I like you a little, Perry, but I don't want to get married now. When I get married, I want—'

He waited, but she did not finish.

'What do you want, Lily? I'll give you everything you want. Tell me what it is. I'll do anything for you, Lily, no matter what it is. All you have to do is tell me, Lily.'

She buried her face against him and shook her head.

'I don't know what I want—it's just something—I don't know exactly what.'

'Won't you try to tell me what it is, Lily? If you told me, I'd do something about it. I'll do anything for you, Lily.'

'I want to be different,' she said quickly. 'I don't want to be like Mama—I don't want to live like her—and be like she is.'

55

'You don't have to be like her, Lily. If we went away, you'd live the way you wanted to. That's why—'

'But I'm afraid I will be like her—that's what I'm afraid of —I want to be different.'

The door was flung open and the lights switched on. They both sat up, momentarily blinded by the unaccustomed light. As soon as Perry recognized Molly, he jumped to his feet. She had already started towards him, and when he saw the look on her face, he ran to the window and jumped out before she could reach him. Then, while she stood above him in the window, he backed away as fast as he could and ran off into the night.

Molly turned and walked slowly across the room until she was standing over Lily.

'I caught you, didn't I?' she said angrily.

'I wasn't doing anything, Mama.'

'Wasn't doing anything! What was Perry Trotter doing in here then?'

'Nothing. He climbed through the window. But I didn't tell him to come here.'

'You don't have to tell them. Why didn't you make him leave?'

'I tried to, Mama, but he wouldn't go.'

'You didn't try very hard.' Molly sat down on the bed, her shoulders drooping and her hands falling listlessly to her lap. 'You're too much like me—that's the whole trouble. It's the same thing happening all over again. I knew it would sooner or later. It was bound to. I don't know what to do about it. Maybe Lucy Trotter was right after all. I'm not raising you the way you ought to grow up. It's not right. You'll end up just like me. It's all my fault. You ought to have a better mother to look after you.' She began to cry. 'I don't know what to do. I wish I was dead—then you wouldn't grow up to be like me. It's all my fault—I wish I was dead!'

Molly put her hands over her face and sobbed. Lily tried to comfort her by putting her arms around her mother's shoulders. They clung to each other for a long time.

'I've just got to get you married,' Molly said, shaking herself with determination. 'That's the only hope. I've just got to get you married. If I don't, I know just as sure as the sun rises Wednesday morning what'll happen.'

'But I don't want to get married yet, Mama,' Lily protested. 'I want to wait a while, Mama. Please don't make me!'

'Why not?'

'I don't know anybody I want to marry, Mama. I don't want to marry Perry Trotter and—'

'You don't have to marry Perry Trotter. There'll be somebody else.'

'Who?'

'I don't know yet, but it'll be somebody else. We'll find him. I've made up my mind to that and nothing's going to stop me. It'd be dangerous to put it off any longer. When they start climbing through the window and getting into bed with you, that's a sure sign it's time to get busy and find somebody to marry you. I know all about it, and I'm not going to take any chances. Either you'll get married or else you'll end up even worse than me.'

'Suppose Perry comes back,' Lily said. 'I can't make him stay away. He'll want to come back again.'

'I'll attend to that,' Molly told her. She got up and went to the door. 'Now, you do just like I tell you after this. I know how to handle them when they are as persistent as Perry Trotter.'

She opened the door and walked squarely into Jethro, who had been listening to what was being said. He looked confused when he suddenly found himself confronted by Molly and he quickly stepped backward out of her way.

'What are you up to, Jethro?' she demanded angrily.

'Who, me?'

'Yes, you!'

'Oh, I was just looking around for a place to sleep,' he said, his face breaking into a grin. 'Looks like there ain't but two beds in the whole house, and I don't know which way to look for a place to sleep.'

Jethro was standing on his toes and peering over Molly's shoulder at Lily. Molly reached back and pulled the door shut.

'Of course, now, I ain't used to nothing special,' he said, 'because over there in Woodbine County I had a little old make-shift place, but I would like to stretch out somewhere that's

57

halfway comfortable. However, anything that was good enough for Putt'll be good enough for me.'

Molly pushed him down the hall.

'I'll fix you a pallet on the parlour floor,' she told him. 'You go in there and wait while I get out the quilts.'

Jethro was perched on the edge of the red sofa when Molly came in and spread the quilts on the floor. He slipped off his overall straps and unlaced his shoes. When he straightened up, Molly had left. He took off his overalls, leaving on his shirt, and lay down on the pallet and pulled the quilt up to his chin. He lay there for the next half-hour listening to Molly's movements in the room across the hall and shivering in the cool night air. He stood it as long as he could before getting up to look for an additional quilt. Then he got up and tiptoed down the hall past Molly's room to Lily's door. Carefully turning the knob, he hastily stepped inside and closed the door noiselessly. Lily's light was burning and she had turned on the radio again. He stood there looking at her for several moments before she knew he was in the room. Jethro's snaggle-toothed grin spread over his face.

'What do you want, Uncle Jethro?' Lily asked him.

He crossed the room.

'You know, it gets downright chilly here at night,' he said, hugging himself with his arms. 'I'm near about froze.'

Lily suddenly burst into laughter.

'What's so funny?' he asked.

Just then he heard Molly's feet hit the floor in the next room. He was backing toward the door when she ran into the room. Lily was still laughing, and as soon as she saw her mother she began pointing at Jethro.

'Look at Uncle Jethro, Mama! Look how funny he looks in his shirt tail!'

Jethro, frowning, looked down at his thin spindly legs protruding from the bottom of his shirt. He quickly drew his shirt tightly around his stomach.

'I never did like to be laughed at,' he protested, looking at Molly. She glared at him angrily. 'Now, maybe I ain't much to look at, but—'

Molly almost jerked him off his feet when she reached out and caught him by the arm. He found himself being pushed and shoved down the hall toward the parlour. He did not have an opportunity to say a word until he found himself backed up against the parlour table. Molly, with hands on hips, regarded him with a cold unrelenting stare.

'I was froze plumb stiff, Molly,' he said in an earnest manner. 'I lay there on that pallet, shaking like a hant. I just had to get up and go look for more cover. I just had to, I tell you.'

'Then why didn't you ask me for it, instead of going down there to her room?'

'You've already put yourself out so much on my account, I just hated to bother you about a little thing like that.'

Instead of answering, Molly sat down on the red sofa and looked at him thoughtfully. Jethro stood in the middle of the room hugging his shirt tail against his stomach and shivering all over.

'There's only one thing to do, and that's to keep an eye on you.' She looked at him for another moment and then got up and went across the hall to her room. When she turned around, Jethro was there. 'Go get your pallet,' she said in an exasperated voice, 'and put it in here where I can watch you.'

Jethro obediently brought his pallet and spread it on the bedroom floor. Saying nothing more, Molly put out the light and got into bed. Jethro lay on the floor listening to every sound in the room and wondering how long it would be before Molly fell asleep. It was not long before he began to shiver with cold again. He drew his knees up against his chest, rolled the quilts around his doubled-up body, and waited. After another half-hour he got up and felt his way in the dark room to the bed. He could not see Molly's face, and he did not know she was still awake until he got into the bed with her. She moved over unprotestingly while he snuggled against the warmth of her body. He waited a while before saying anything.

'I sure do appreciate a nice warm place to sleep,' he said in a contented voice at last. 'I don't know nothing worse than a shivery pallet on a cold floor. It just never was my nature to get used to sleeping like that.'

Molly made no reply and, encouraged by her silence, he snuggled closer and warmed his cold feet against the bulging calves of her legs.

59

'Over there in Woodbine County I had me a little cot in a shanty where the cold wind blew near about all winter long,' he said reminiscently, 'and it wasn't much better in the summer time, neither. The nights over there are just as chillish in summer as they is over here. The folks I worked for wouldn't give me but two old quilts to keep me warm, and I had to pile a lot of tow-sacks on top of me to keep from freezing. Over here, though,' he added, snuggling against Molly, 'I'll be content just like I am now. I don't know no better way to keep warm in chilly weather. I wish now I'd come over here a lot sooner.'

Molly lay quietly, still saying nothing, and Jethro began to feel so good he could not go to sleep. He lay there for several minutes while he told himself how lucky he was, and after that he made up his mind never to go back to Woodbine County.

He was thoroughly warm by then, and he began to be restless. Molly turned over.

'I want you to promise me something, Jethro,' she said, speaking slowly and deliberately.

'I'll sure do that for you, Molly,' he agreed without hesitation. 'I promise for sure.'

'I want you to promise to leave Lily alone, Jethro.'

Jethro did not answer as quickly as she had hoped he would.

'Did you hear what I said?' she said, shaking him.

'I reckon I did,' he replied.

'Are you going to promise that?'

'Never, at no time at all?'

'Not at any time.'

'I ought to think about that for a minute, first. She's mighty pert, and I wouldn't want to make no misstatement.'

Molly sat up, breathing heavily. 'You'd better make up your mind in a hurry, Jethro Bowser,' she warned him.

'Well, I reckon I could promise that, if it's what you want me to say.'

Molly lay down again with a weary sigh.

'But I never was one to make a promise if I didn't mean to stick to it,' he continued. 'I hate to go so far as to make promises. I'd a heap rather just go ahead and tell myself I wasn't going to do something, unless I was compelled to change my mind later on.'

Molly jumped out of bed and switched on the light. Before he knew what was happening, she had grabbed him by the arm and flung him to the floor. He lay there at her feet and looked up at her in surprise.

'I don't care if you are Putt's brother,' she shouted. 'That's one thing I won't stand for. I'll kill you right here and now if I think you'd bother her. I'd kill any man who did, until she gets married to somebody.'

Molly turned and went to the other side of the room in search of something she could strike him with if necessary. When she picked up the china washbowl, Jethro hastily got to his feet and retreated behind the bed.

'If I ever caught you bothering her, I'd kill you as quick as I would a mite,' she told him threateningly. Jethro, clutching his shirt tail against his stomach, began to tremble with cold and fear. 'The first time I ever caught a man in bed with her I shot at him, but he managed to get away alive. The next time he won't, though. I'll see to that.'

'I didn't mean it like you took it, Molly. Honest to God, I didn't. I was just sort of speculating about it, that's all. A man likes to speculate about something like that. It just seems like the natural thing to do. I know now it's the last thing I'd do as long as I live. That's something you ought to believe, Molly. I wouldn't tell you no lie at a time like this. I sure wouldn't!'

Molly sat down on the side of the bed and looked at him as if she were unable to make up her mind whether or not to believe him. Jethro stayed where he was, keeping the bed between them, in case she should suddenly change her mind and make a lunge at him.

'I never would have said what I did this while ago if I'd known you'd take it like that, Molly. I was just talking along out loud to myself like I always do when I'm thinking deep about a matter. If there's one thing in this world I ain't going to do, it's doing what you was talking about. That's God's own truth, Molly.'

Molly looked at him with a searching gaze for a few moments

longer, and then she got into bed and pulled up the cover. Jethro, afraid to move, stayed where he was and shook all over.

'Turn out that light, Jethro,' he heard her say at last.

Obediently, Jethro turned out the light as quickly as he could.

Chapter 7

AFTER a restless night Molly was more determined than ever to get Lily married and out of the house as soon as possible. She spent the morning selecting the best-looking clothes she and Lily possessed and early that afternoon they left the house and walked downtown. First they strolled slowly around the courthouse square while Molly was determinedly eliminating the men she dismissed as being financially unworthy of Lily. That immediately removed as prospects the crowd of men and boys lounging in front of the poolroom and listening to baseball scores being broadcast over the radio. There was a row of lawyers' offices on the north side of the square, but Molly was suspicious of all lawyers and she unhesitatingly avoided them. There were several doctors and dentists in town, but they were elderly and married, like Doc Logan, and besides, they were always so busy in their offices that there was no opportunity to see them without making appointments far in advance. Molly had already decided that doctors were poor risks, anyway, because the only one she knew was Doc Logan, who would promise a girl anything but who had remained married to his wife for twenty years. She was also quick to eliminate the store clerks and soda jerkers, and after that she began to worry. She had no use for farmers, because she had nothing but bitter memories of her own life on farms and she wanted to keep Lily away from the country. By that time she had narrowed down the possibilities to the point where there were few men left. Worried and discouraged, she took Lily into the drugstore on the corner and they sat down and ordered chocolate sodas.

They sat there for half an hour sipping their sodas while Molly frantically tried to think what to do next. She had made Lily sit at the table facing the door and soda fountain so she would be instantly seen by men who came in and stood at the fount for a quick coke, and she herself turned around to see who had entered each time the door swung open. Lily's long dark hair had been brushed until it gleamed and sparkled in the light and occasionally the soda jerkers caught a glimpse of Lily's black lace step-ins when she re-crossed her legs. One of the soda jerkers, who had been watching Lily ever since she came in, winked at her several times, but Molly nudged her and told her not to do anything to encourage him.

'There's more riff-raff in this town than sparrows on a gin-house roof,' Molly said, shaking her head with discouragement. 'There's so much of it these days that a woman wastes half her lifetime trying to find a man who's worth-while to marry. It's getting so bad nowadays that most women just have to take what they can get—and just look at what they do get most of the time! Just look at those boys jerking soda. I'll bet you not a single one of them has a dime left over after a Saturday night binge down in the Hollow. If you married one of them, you'd go begging on the streets by the time the sun rose Wednesday morning.'

'But they're young yet, Mama,' Lily said. 'They won't always work in drugstores. They'll get better jobs when they're older.'

'Maybe some will, but right now if you married one of them you'd be worse off than I am. I want to find a man with real money to marry you. Somebody like—well, like a man who works in a bank.' She stopped and her eyes opened wide and she smiled to herself. 'That's where the real money is—in a bank. Do you know anybody who works in the bank, honey?'

Lily thought for a moment.

'Claude Stevens works in the bank,' she told Molly.

'Who's he?'

'His uncle owns the bank, and he's about twenty-five or twenty-seven, and he's awfully good-looking, too.'

'Is he already married, honey?'

Lily shook her head. 'But I think he's engaged to Bessie Allbright.'

'That's nothing,' Molly said with a significant look. 'I was

64

engaged seven times, and married once.' She immediately picked up her purse and pushed back her chair. 'The only time an engagement really truly counts is when it leads to the other thing. Come on, honey.'

'Where are we going now, Mama?'

'Let's walk past the bank,' she said, beckoning to Lily with an agitated gesture.

They left the drugstore and strolled down the street toward the bank. Just before reaching the building, Molly stopped and inspected her dim reflection in a display window. After that she held herself erectly and fixed a smile upon her face. They walked slowly past the bank several times, and on each occasion Molly turned her head and looked intently through the window.

'Is he in there, honey?' she asked excitedly. 'Did you see him?'

Lily nodded.

'We'd better hurry and go in before they close up, honey. It's almost three o'clock already. Now, you just stay right with me.'

'What are we going to do when we get inside, Mama?'

'We're going inside to see this fellow who's engaged to Bessie Allbright, of course.'

'Then what will we do, Mama?'

'I don't know yet, but I'll think of something. You nudge me so I'll know him when I see him.'

'Please don't do anything embarrassing, Mama,' Lily said nervously. 'Don't come right out and say things you shouldn't.'

'I know how to get next to a man and make it look as natural as the sun rising Wednesday morning. I haven't lived as long as I have around men without learning that.'

They walked into the bank and went to one of the high desks against the wall.

'Now, which one is Claude Stevens?' Molly asked in a hoarse whisper.

'He's the one at the third window, down there,' Lily whispered in reply.

'He looks like a good man,' Molly said with a quick nod. 'A man who keeps his hair combed as neat as he does is usually worth any trouble you want to go to. These shaggy-haired men like your Uncle Jethro are always unreliable. Now, you do just

65

like I tell you, honey. We'll go up there and I'll start talking to him about something or other. Then in a little while I'll remember something I've got to attend to right away and I'll leave. You stay there and talk to him and see what kind of an interest he'll take in you.'

'But suppose he doesn't take any interest in me at all, Mama.' Lily clutched her mother's arm. 'What can I do then? I wouldn't know what to say.'

'How do you get any man to do what you want him to do?' Molly said with an impatient frown.

Lily was distressed. 'I'm afraid, Mama,' she whispered in a quavering voice. 'Please don't go away and leave me standing there all alone!'

'There're some things you have to do all by yourself, honey,' she said sympathetically. 'Marrying's one of them. You know that by now.' She pushed Lily forward. 'Come on.'

Claude Stevens looked up and smiled in a businesslike manner. Molly placed her arm on the teller's window and leaned as close to him as she could.

'What can I do for you, Mrs. Bowser?' he asked.

Molly smiled and tried to appear casual as she looked into her purse. After a long search she closed it and put it back under her arm.

'Lily and I had a little banking matter to transact,' she said, fully at ease, 'but I'm afraid I left it at home. I'll bring it down the next time Lily and I come downtown.'

'I'll be very glad to take care of it for you, Mrs. Bowser,' he said. He glanced from Molly to Lily. Lily broke into a hasty smile. 'It's a nice day today, isn't it?'

'It's a humdinger of a day,' Molly spoke up before Lily could say anything.

Lily, smiling self-consciously, nodded to Claude. There was a period of silence during which Molly reached down and caught Lily's skirt and tried to make her come closer to the teller's window. Claude rustled a stack of papers.

'Have you been well lately, Mrs. Bowser?' he asked.

'Oh, my!' Molly exclaimed excitedly. 'I just happened to think! I left something in the store down the street a few minutes ago. I'll have to run and find it before it's lost for good.' She caught Lily's arm and jerked her roughly toward the window. 'It'd be a calamity if I lost it!' She reached down and pinched Lily's hip. 'Lily, don't mind me—I've got to run!'

'But, Mama—' Lily said, trembling.

When she turned around, Molly was going through the door to the street. Claude was watching her curiously when she looked at him again, and she tried to smile.

'Where did she leave it?' he asked.

'I don't know, exactly.'

'It's too bad.'

Lily nodded, and then smiled quickly again.

Claude thought for a moment. 'What was it, anyway?'

'I don't know, exactly,' she said again, unable to think of anything else to say.

Claude was busily clipping sheets of paper together and stacking cheques in a drawer. Lily stood there trying to think of something to say and wondering what Molly would do under the circumstances. Presently Claude leaned forward.

'It's closing time, Lily,' he said.

She caught her breath and tried desperately to think of something to say or do before she was left standing there.

'Will you excuse me for a minute while I take this drawer to the safe?' he continued. 'I'll be right back.'

'You're coming back?'

'I certainly am. Now, don't go away, Lily.'

He picked up the drawer of cheques and greenbacks and started toward the safe. All the customers had left the bank and the janitor was pulling down the shades. There was no way for Molly to get back into the bank now that it had closed for the day, and Lily wondered what she should do. She was still trying to think of something when Claude walked through the waist-high swinging door at the rear of the building.

'I'm all finished for the day, Lily,' he said, swinging his hat in his hand. 'Why don't we go up to the drugstore and have a drink while you wait for your mother?'

'I'd love to,' she said, relieved.

Claude unlocked the front door, let them out, and relocked it. They looked down the street for a moment, but Molly was nowhere within sight, and after that they walked slowly up the street toward the drugstore on the corner.

After they had sat down in a booth and had ordered drinks, Lily felt at ease for the first time. She leaned forward, resting her elbows on the table, and smiled at Claude.

'It's such a thrill to be sitting here with you, Claude,' she said shyly. 'I never dreamed of anything like this happening to me. I didn't think you'd ever noticed me.'

'You'd be surprised if you knew the number of times I've watched you walk along the street in front of the bank.'

'Really? Why did you do that, Claude?'

'How could anybody keep from looking at you, Lily?'

'There're a lot of girls in town much better looking than I am.'

'I don't know about that. But anyway, there's something about you, Lily, that attracts looks. It would be hard for a man to keep from looking at you when he has the chance.'

Lily leaned closer, resting both arms on the table. She could see without raising her eyes that Claude was watching her intently. She did not want to say anything for fear he would stop looking at her like that, and she leaned further over the table. Claude's fingers were nervously twisting matches from a matchbook.

'I meant everything I said, Lily,' he told her in a low voice.

She looked up, her glance meeting his for the first time, and then quickly lowered her head again.

'I've got my car around the corner,' he said huskily. 'I'd like to drive you home, Lily.'

She started to get up immediately, but she caught herself and waited.

'I don't know,' she said, looking straight into Claude's eyes. 'Mama—'

Claude reached across the table and put his hand on hers.

'Maybe she's got something else to do,' he suggested hopefully. 'Maybe she's not ready to go home yet.'

'I guess it'd be all right then,' she agreed.

Claude stood up and dropped some change on the table. While they were walking to the door, she could see with a side-long glance that the two soda jerkers were whispering to each other as they watched her leave. She and Claude walked in

68

silence around the corner to the parking lot and got into his car. Claude drove rapidly through the square, but instead of turning up Muscadine Street, he went straight ahead toward the country. They drove for a quarter of an hour before either of them spoke. He slowed down the car.

'I really meant every word I said, Lily,' he told her. 'You believe that, don't you?'

'What did you say, Claude?' she asked, moving closer to him. 'Tell me again.'

Claude suddenly stopped the car by the side of the road and put his arms around her. As she closed her eyes she felt her lips crushed against his.

'You still haven't told me, Claude,' she whispered when he released her.

'You're wonderful to look at, Lily,' he said quickly. 'You're wonderful to see on the street,-but it's a lot nicer to have you here like this.'

She wanted to ask him about Bessie Allbright, but she decided to wait until some other time.

'I guess it looks odd for us to be parked out here in the country in broad daylight,' he said, laughing a little.

'I like being here, Claude, even if it is daytime,' she told him promptly.

'Me, too,' he said, drawing her closer. They clung to each other for a long time. 'Could I come to see you, Lily?' he asked awkwardly. 'I mean, would it be all right?'

'You mean at night?'

'Of course—that's what I mean.'

'Well,' she said slowly, trying not to appear to be too eager to have him come to see her at night, 'I guess it'd be all right.'

He drew her close to him and kissed her for a long time. Her heart was beating so violently that she felt that she could not stand it much longer. She was breathless when he finally released her. They had been there for almost an hour and the sun was sinking.

'Maybe we'd better go,' he said. 'It's getting late.'

They drove back to town in silence. Lily sat close beside him, wondering if he would really come to see her as he had said he wanted to. She wanted to ask him about Bessie Allbright, but she was still afraid to mention Bessie's name.

Claude stopped the car in front of the bungalow, got out, and opened the door for her.

'Won't you come in for just a little while, Claude?' she said invitingly.

He went as far as the porch with her and stopped.

'We could go inside, Claude.' She touched his hand with her fingers. 'I don't know if Mama's back yet, or not.'

He followed her into the parlour and sat down beside her on the red sofa. She let him kiss her for a long time, and then she kissed him. Neither of them knew that Molly was standing at the door until they heard her speak.

'I didn't know you were back yet, you and Claude,' Molly said in a pleased manner. 'Now, you two go right ahead with what you were talking about. I'm going right out and you can have the whole house to yourselves.'

Claude cleared his throat and loosened his collar with his finger. He glanced, embarrassed, at Lily.

'Did you find it, Mrs. Bowser?' he asked her.

'Find what?' she said.

'Whatever it was you lost downtown this afternoon.'

'Oh that! It was right where I left it.'

'That's fine,' he said, watching her questioningly. 'I'm glad it wasn't gone when you went back for it.'

'So am I,' she agreed heartily.

Claude looked at Lily for a moment and then back at Molly.

'What was it, anyway?' he asked, unable to conceal his curiosity any longer.

A startled look passed between Molly and Lily. It was several moments before Molly could think of what to say.

'Oh, it was nothing of importance,' she said, trying to make her reply sound casual. 'It had a little sentimental value, that's all.'

She turned and started down the hall.

'Now, you two go right ahead with what you were talking about,' she called over her shoulder. 'And don't forget that the whole house is yours. I'm going out for a while.'

'What was it your mother lost, anyway?' Claude asked per-

70

sistently. 'She was so worried when she left the bank that I was afraid she wouldn't find it.'

'Mama's always losing little trinkets,' she said, smiling up at him temptingly. 'When do you want to see me again, Claude?'

Chapter 8

MOLLY knew something was wrong the moment she saw the grave expression on Reverend Bigbee's face. While they were walking silently into the parlour and sitting down, she was sure that he had found out about her visit with Christine while he was out of town and certain that he had come to forbid her to see Christine again. Ordinarily Reverend Bigbee was friendly in appearance and smiled easily if he thought the occasion called for light levity, but today the corners of his mouth drooped disapprovingly and his long chin hung from his face with a sorrowful sag. This time he looked exactly like he did when he was conducting a funeral service. Being tall and dark-complexioned with coarse black hair that hung in a forelock over his left eye, he was endowed with the ability to adjust his mobile features upon a moment's notice to the gaiety of a wedding reception, and half an hour later have them conform to the solemn atmosphere of a funeral on a rainy afternoon. As her pastor, he had come to call on Molly previously, but this was his first visit since Putt's death and, instead of being comforting and sympathetic as she had expected him to be under the circumstances, he was treating her as though she were a member of some other church. Molly was positive by then that Reverend Bigbee had become suspicious and had found out from Mamie that she and Christine had smoked cigarettes and given each other vitamin injections one whole afternoon.

'I want to pray for you, Mrs. Bowser,' he said solemnly, breaking the silence and filling the parlour with the awesome sound of his voice. 'The time has come to relieve the torment of your sinful soul. Let us pray, Mrs. Bowser.'

Molly trembled to think that he was at last leading up to a violent denunciation of her and she wondered how much longer it would be before he finally got around to mentioning her visit with Christine. She nodded uncertainly, but at the same time anxious to get the matter over with.

'I'd like to hear a nice comforting prayer, Reverend Bigbee,' she told him, 'but just the same I haven't done anything really truly sinful.'

His jaw dropped with astonishment as he stared at Molly's innocent-looking face. He had been the pastor of the church for the past five years and he performed almost all of the marriage ceremonies and conducted most of the funeral services in town. The Baptists had a pastor, but he came to Agricola to preach only on the third Sunday of the month and, consequently, was poorly acquainted with the people and their misdeeds. Reverend Bigbee, on the other hand, made it a practice to keep himself fully informed of the people's misdeeds, members and non-members alike. What he did not hear at the barbershop and elsewhere in town, Lucy Trotter heard about directly from the women of the church, who generally were able to give her the information in greater detail than he could hear himself, and she lost no time in passing the information along to Reverend Bigbee. In that way, very little happened in Agricola that he did not know enough about to use as the springboard for a sermon. Only recently Jim Hathaway's second cousin, Fanny Fellows, came to visit Jim and his wife, and Mrs. Hathaway phoned for the police at two o'clock in the morning to come to the house and arrest Fanny. Jim said he and Fanny were only sitting in the back yard drinking beer, but his wife was positive there was more to it than that and she had Fanny arrested and locked up over the week-end, anyway. That happened on a Friday night, and on Sunday morning Reverend Bigbee preached a strongly worded sermon against drinking beer with unmarried relatives of the opposite sex. He said he felt it was his duty to stay tuned to the times in order to rout out contemporary sin. Jim Hathaway said he was an old busybody and threatened to join the Baptist Church, but Reverend Bigbee had a long talk with him and prayed for him, and Jim finally agreed to stay in the Methodist Church and thereafter to do his best to overcome his bad habits.

73

Molly waited tensely while Reverend Bigbee fixed his solemn gaze midway between his and Molly's chairs.

'I didn't mean to discourage you from praying for me, Reverend Bigbee,' she told him uneasily. 'I always did like to hear a preacher say prayers. It sounds so different than listening to an ordinary somebody pray.'

She could see him glance up at her from beneath his heavy black brows as he sat there silently phrasing and rephrasing what he was about to say.

'Mrs. Bowser,' he began in a deep tone, his face taking on once more the expression he usually reserved for graveside funeral services, 'Mrs. Bowser, I always had a deep and abiding respect for your late husband. He was a fine, God-fearing man. He was a staunch supporter of the church. If he was here today I'm sure he'd approve of what I'm about to say.'

Tears filled Molly's eyes to overflowing and dripped down her cheeks.

'I'll never be the same again after losing Putt,' she began sobbing a little. 'The bottom just dropped out of the bucket when Putt went.'

'I feel deeply sorry for you, Mrs. Bowser,' he spoke up, lifting his voice above the sound of her sobs, 'and you have my heart-felt sympathy. However, I—'

'Nobody knows how hard it is for a poor middle-aged widow to get along in the world, Reverend Bigbee. A widow like me has to wear some mourning, pay the rent, and at the same time keep her eyes open in the right direction if she's ever to find a man to take her late husband's place. Men are few and far between when it comes to marrying, and a poor middle-aged widow like me has to be ready at the drop of a hat to grab whatever opportunity comes her way. Sometimes I think life's not worth living any more, because you know yourself it's harder for a somebody like me to find a man than it is for these skinny young widows. I never was attractive like some women are, and a widow my age, on top of everything else, has to scramble like a cat on a ginhouse roof to get a man.'

Reverend Bigbee watched Molly with a helpless droop of his shoulders. His hands dropped listlessly over the arms of the chair. He stared down at the floor when he saw Molly raise her hand to dab at her tear-soaked eyes with her handkerchief.

'The world doesn't make provision for a widow like me at all, Reverend Bigbee. People expect her to get along somehow, no matter how poor she is. If she can't find a man to marry her, she has to do something else for a living, and if she can't make a living one way, they expect her to make it some other way, and then they all blame her and call her a dreadful sinner if she goes ahead and does the best she can.' She stopped and looked at the expression on Reverend Bigbee's face. 'Maybe you've run across widows like me before, Reverend Bigbee.'

'No, I don't think I ever did.'

'But you wouldn't blame me for getting along the best I can, would you, Reverend Bigbee?'

He was silent for a while.

'That's what I came to see you about, Mrs. Bowser,' he said, getting down on his knees and resting his arms on the seat of the chair. 'We'd better pray now.'

Molly eased her enormously heavy body into a kneeling position and waited expectantly.

'O Lord,' he began, turning his head slightly to one side so he could open his eyes from time to time and watch Molly, 'O Lord, help us with the problem of this poor widow. She lost her husband in an awful accident and has been mourning him ever since. Now the time's come when something's got to be done. She's living a life of sin, but she wants to give it up right away. Her late husband's brother moved in, and—'

'You must be talking about Jethro,' Molly interrupted.

'That's right, Mrs. Bowser.'

'Who told you about Jethro?'

'Everybody in town knows—'

'But who came out and mentioned it?'

'One of the good women of my congregation, Mrs. Bowser.'

'Was it Lucy Trotter?'

'I believe she did speak to me about it this morning.'

'I knew it!' she said angrily. 'It's none of Lucy Trotter's business. She'd better keep her nasty nose out of my affairs.'

'Mrs. Bowser, it's all over town by now. Jethro's been saying one thing and another downtown, and that hasn't helped the all-over situation one bit. Everybody knows he moved in here and is living in this same house with you. Mrs. Trotter was only expressing what's common knowledge, and she has a right to be outraged by what's gone on in this house. She said she saw it with her own eyes, and she's a truthful Christian woman.'

'Saw what?'

'She told me she watched you and Jethro Bowser in your room the first day he was here. Naturally, Mrs. Trotter was too modest to go into details, but she said she thought it was her duty to tell me in general what she saw. Now, that can't continue, Mrs. Bowser. I want you and Jethro to marry at once. It can all be done this afternoon.'

'Me marry Jethro Bowser?' she said in astonishment. 'Marry that good-for-nothing scamp?' She began to laugh, 'I'm not that hard up, Reverend Bigbee.'

'It's got to be done, Mrs. Bowser,' he said doggedly. 'It's your Christian duty.'

'If I have to, I'll send him back to Woodbine County, but I sure wouldn't marry him.'

'The sin has to be rectified, Mrs. Bowser. Sending him back to Woodbine County wouldn't cancel out the sin. The only way you can clear yourself of this awful thing is to marry him right away. You and him can go down to the courthouse right now and take out the licence. I'll perform the ceremony as soon as you get back. There won't be any fee, either, under the circumstances.'

'I'm going to tell that Lucy Trotter a thing or two,' she said determinedly. 'I'll give her a piece of my mind.'

'That doesn't change the fact that——'

'If she pulled her shades down and stopped snooping through other folks' windows——'

'I'm a strong-minded man, Mrs. Bowser.' He stood up and walked toward her. 'When I make up my mind to rout out sin, nothing stands in my way. Now, this's a serious matter. Where's Jethro?'

Molly nodded in the direction of the rear of the house. 'He was out there in the back yard digging in the trash pile the last time I saw him,' she said meekly. 'He's either there now or else resting on the back porch.'

Reverend Bigbee strode heavily down the hall to the

back porch. He beckoned to Jethro and walked back up the hall. Jethro, surprised and curious, followed him into the parlour.

'I'm Reverend Bigbee,' he stated abruptly, turning to Jethro and holding out his hand.

Jethro shook hands with him while he looked inquiringly at Molly.

'Mrs. Bowser and I have been talking things over, Jethro,' he said, speaking rapidly, 'and we've come to the conclusion that it would be a good thing—a desirable and necessary thing—if you—if she—if you and she got married right away.'

'I didn't say no such thing!' Molly said indignantly.

Jethro grinned until his snaggled teeth gleamed in his mouth. He swallowed nervously and glanced at Molly.

'I don't mind,' he said, his grin spreading over his face.

'Well, I do!' Molly spoke up.

'Now, Mrs. Bowser,' Reverend Bigbee said hastily, 'this is no time to hem and haw. There's no time to lose.'

'To tell the truth, I've sort of been thinking off and on about getting married,' Jethro told Reverend Bigbee earnestly. 'The only reason I didn't stir around sooner and do something about it was because I couldn't make up my mind if it'd be her or Lily.'

Reverend Bigbee grabbed Jethro's arm and shook him. 'She's the one, Jethro!' he said excitedly, pointing at Molly. 'Not her daughter! No! Not Lily!'

Jethro hung his head and looked at the floor. 'If a man can still make a choice——' he began.

Reverend Bigbee shook him again. 'You're not already married, are you, Jethro? You're a single man, aren't you?'

Jethro jerked his head up and down. 'I'm single, all right. I once asked a widow-woman over in Woodbine County how about me and her getting hitched up, but she backed out in the end. I ain't never had another chance to ask another one to get married since. That's why I don't mind marrying Molly, or Lily, and if it's all the same to you——'

Reverend Bigbee was shaking his head vigorously. 'It's not the same, Jethro. Now, get that out of your mind.'

He glanced shyly at Molly. 'Well,' he said, pulling at his ear, 'it does seem like the natural thing to do, since she's already in the family. If she was good enough for Putt, she'll be good enough for me.'

'Now, Mrs. Bowser,' he said enthusiastically, turning to Molly, 'see how agreeable Jethro is? Why don't you and him hurry down to the courthouse right away, and then I'll——'

'No,' she stated flatly. 'I'm not going to do it.'

'Why not, Mrs. Bowser? Jethro's willing. You just heard him say so.'

'If he was anybody else in the world, I might. But not Jethro Bowser.'

'Why, Mrs. Bowser, why?'

'Because Jethro's too weak-looking in the seat of the pants, that's why. I want me a good man when I remarry. I deserve a good man at my age.'

Reverend Bigbee looked at her helplessly before bowing his head despairingly and walking to the window. He stood there with his back to the room and gazed unhappily at the dusty unpaved street. His shoulders drooped as if his arms and hands had been heavily weighted and his thick dark skin sagged loosely on the frame of his face. It was a long time before he turned around and faced Molly and Jethro again.

'I don't know what to say now,' he told them in despair. 'I'm at my rope's end.' He shook his head despondently. 'The devil holds sway in spite of everything.'

He dropped his body heavily into a chair and held his head in his hands. 'If you will persist in not doing what you know you should, Mrs. Bowser, please do one thing for me.'

'What is it, Reverend Bigbee?' she asked brightly.

'Make him sleep by himself in another room.' He took his hands from his head and looked at Molly with a pleading expression. 'That's the least you can do under the circumstances, Mrs. Bowser—the very least!'

'I wouldn't want to do that.'

'Why, Mrs. Bowser, why?'

'Because if I let him sleep with me, I know where he is every minute and don't have to worry and be jumping up all night to see if he's got in bed with Lily. As soon as I can get

Lily married off, then I'll put him out and make him sleep by himself.'

'This is worse than I thought,' he said, shaking his head. 'It's getting worse all the time.' He frowned harshly at Jethro. 'Why don't you go back where you came from?'

'What for? I like it a lot better over here than I did over in Woodbine County. Something's going on over here all the time. Over there nothing much ever happened at all. No, sir, I wouldn't want to leave here now.'

Reverend Bigbee gazed down at his clenched hands as though he hoped to find in them some solution. 'About Lily, Mrs. Bowser. Is there any chance of her getting married right away?'

'I'm working as hard as I ever did about anything in my life. I'm a lot more particular about her than I am about my own self, and that makes it harder. I wouldn't want to see her marry just anybody who came along, like Jethro, there. I want her to marry a rich man.'

'Is there anybody—I mean, do you have anybody in particular in mind?'

'Claude Stevens looks like he'd make a good man for her. And he's rich, too.'

'But Claude Stevens is engaged to marry Mrs. Allbright's daughter, Bessie,' he said, distressed to hear what Molly proposed. 'Their engagement was announced a few weeks ago, and Mrs. Allbright has already spoken to me about having a church wedding. It would be a terrible thing to break up that match. Mrs. Allbright would be sure to think I had something to do with it. She's one of our strongest church members, too.'

'I've got my worries, let her have hers. If Claude Stevens wants to marry Lily, Bessie Allbright can get out and look for somebody else.'

Discouraged and weary, Reverend Bigbee got up and started toward the door. 'I'll have to go now, Mrs. Bowser,' he told her. 'I'll think about it and pray over it, and I hope I can find the answer. When I do, I'll come back and talk to you about it. In the meantime——' he turned and glared at Jethro. 'In the meantime I earnestly hope you'll find some other place for him to sleep, if he won't go away.'

79

He gravely shook hands with Molly and then with Jethro and, without another word, walked out of the house.

Molly sank wearily into a chair.

'What a life for the female element,' she said to Jethro.

Chapter 9

JETHRO did not come home at suppertime and Molly was angry and disappointed when she and Lily sat down to eat, because she had planned on getting him out on the back porch after dark and talking to him about giving her some more money. So far, all she had had from him was the ten dollars she had managed to make him give her the first day he was there. For the past several days he had spent most of the time downtown talking to the men in the poolroom and around the depot and trying to discover if Putt had left any saleable property other than his rubber boots and push cart, both of which Jethro had already found and sold.

'It looks like there's always a no-account somebody in every family, and it looks to me like Jethro's the one in the Bowser family. Putt was a hard-working man, even if he didn't get rich doing what he did. He would never've been caught loafing around the stores like Jethro's doing.'

Lily hurriedly finished eating and went to her room to get ready for her date with Claude Stevens. After she had left the kitchen, Molly spent the next half-hour noisily banging dishes in the sink and slamming the cooking pans on the stove and table, and at the same time listening for the sound of Jethro's coming into the house. She was already thoroughly provoked with Jethro and had made up her mind to tell him what she thought of him when he did come home.

Claude came at eight o'clock and Lily was not ready. Molly heard him on the front porch and, thinking it might be Jethro, she went to the door. Claude said he would wait for Lily on the porch, but Molly persuaded him to come into the parlour. They went inside and sat down. Molly was so glad to know that he had not lost interest in Lily that she began talking excitedly. She talked so rapidly that Claude had no opportunity to say anything and all he could do was to nod his head from time to time.

'Lily always was such a sweet devoted child,' she said with an excited flourish of her hands. 'She's never once given me a minute's trouble since the day she was born. She knows how to take care of herself with any man and I don't have to worry about that. I always said she'd grow up to make some man a fine wife, because she's so considerate and thoughtful about even the littlest things and never acts selfish and asks for more than the average girl wants. She's always cheerful when she gets up in the morning and never goes around grumbling and snarly like some women. Men appreciate that in a wife. Besides all that, she likes to go to the trouble of doing little out-of-the-way things for a man, and that's something else a husband really truly appreciates. A lot of women act as dumb as a cat on a ginhouse roof when they're alone with a man—but not Lily. I've brought her up to know what a man expects of her and she'll make her husband a necessary woman. Of course, I hate to lose Lily, but that's just being downright selfish, because I want her to go ahead and marry and settle down comfortably.'

Claude fingered the brim of his hat and nodded each time Molly looked straight at him and expected him to nod in agreement. He still had not had an opportunity to say anything, but he was glad of that, because so far he had not been able to think of anything appropriate to say under the circumstances.

'Lily's always been very popular with the men, both the young and the middle-yeared, and it looks like age doesn't matter at all as far as she's concerned. They all take to her like sparrows to a ginhouse roof. I've tried to have her associate with only the highest type of men, of course. Ever since she first took an interest in men I've tried to teach her that it's just as easy to take up with a rich man as it is with a poor man and that a rich man appreciates a good time just as much as a poor man, and she's learned by now that a rich man can do more for her in the long run than the other kind. That's what I mean by the highest type. Lots of girls don't have that training and they

82

live to regret it. Lily's been taught, and she won't be holding back around you. That's one thing you don't have to worry about.'

Molly stopped abruptly. Somebody had come up on the front porch and was walking to the door. She was sure it was Jethro and she wanted to keep him out of sight while Claude was there.

'Excuse me, please,' she said hurriedly as she got up and went to the porch.

It was Perry Trotter instead of Jethro. Perry started to say something, but she put her hand over his mouth and led him down the steps and around the house to the back yard. They stood there with her hand over his mouth until she heard Claude and Lily get into the car and drive away. Then she released Perry and sat down on the steps.

'What's the matter, Mrs. Bowser?' he whispered. 'Why'd you bring me around here like that?'

'What did you come over here again for, Perry?' she asked, taking a deep breath. 'What do you want?'

'I want to see Lily.'

'Can't you see Lily's too busy to bother with you?'

'Why is she too busy, Mrs. Bowser?'

'Because she's got a lot of things on her mind.'

'But I like Lily a lot, Mrs. Bowser. Why can't I see her?'

'It's a godforsaken shame you're not ten years older with money in the bank,' she said as she watched him.

'I'm old enough to like Lily now, Mrs. Bowser. I don't have to be any older to like her, do I?'

Molly got up and walked up the steps.

'Right now you're nothing but a pesky pest, Perry,' she told him. 'Go on away and leave us alone.'

She left him standing forlornly in the yard and went into the house to wait for Jethro to come home. After pouring herself a tumblerful of wine she undressed and put on her green dressing-gown and stretched out on the bed. It was after nine o'clock by then and she tried to think what could be keeping Jethro downtown so late at night. He was usually there at mealtime and he had never stayed out so late before. She poured herself some more wine and propped the pillows under her head.

83

She had just made herself comfortable when she heard some-body on the front porch again. Getting up, she ran the comb through her hair and hurried to the porch. It was Perry Trotter once more.

'What do you want this time, Perry?' she said in a disagree-able manner. 'I told you once tonight already to go on away and leave us alone. What's got into you, anyway?'

'I've just got to see Lily, Mrs. Bowser,' he said persistently. 'I've just got to, Mrs. Bowser.'

'What makes you keep on saying you've got to see Lily?' she demanded.

'Well, it's just because I want to, that's why. I can't keep from liking Lily, and I never have a chance to see her. Every time I come over here you make me go away.'

'The thing for you to do is find yourself another girl, Perry. Go worry somebody else till you get what you want. It'll be easy for you at your age. If you'd do that, you'd get it out of your system. Lily's not going to waste her time on you when she's got bigger plans in mind. She's got a date tonight with a man who wants to marry her and give her everything she wants. I wouldn't be at all surprised if they got married any day now.'

'Who is he?' Perry said sullenly.

'Never mind about names. I've told you all you need to know.' She looked at Perry for a moment. 'It'll be a lot better if you forgot all about Lily and quit coming over here. First thing you know you'll ruin Lily's chances of marrying a very high-class man.'

'I'll kill him, that's what I'll do,' he said desperately. 'I'm not scared. I'll kill him so he can't marry Lily.'

He dug his hands defiantly into his pockets.

'You're joking, Perry,' Molly said with a nervous laugh. 'You don't mean that.'

'I'm not going to let anybody else have Lily.'

Molly was worried.

'Come on in the house and let me tell you something, Perry,' she said as she reached out and took him by the arm.

Perry held back at first, but she urged him again, and he followed her through the doorway. She turned and closed the

84

door behind her, and Perry blinked with amazement at the sight of her wide flaring hips and heavy protruding breasts. He tried to get his hand on the door knob, but Molly pulled him away from it.

'What's the matter, Perry?' she said, putting her arm around him and taking him into the parlour.

'I'm—I'm—scared, Mrs. Bowser.'

'There's nothing to be scared about, Perry.' She took him to the red sofa and drew him down beside her. 'You're big enough not to be scared.' She put both arms around him and held him so tightly that he could not move. 'There're just lots of girls who'd like you, Perry. You could have yourself a different girl every night if you wanted to. You don't have to waste all your time on just one in particular. Why don't you go see some of the others?'

'I'm—I'm—afraid,' he said, fighting for breath.

She pulled him closer and he tried to break her grip, but his efforts to get away from her only made Molly squeeze him harder and harder. When she pulled him forward, he kicked and squirmed, but he could not make her stop. He lay there until he felt his face sink into the soft mountainous flesh of her body. His head was swimming dizzily. After a while he stopped kicking and squirming and opened his eyes. He was surprised to find that Molly was no longer holding him, and he raised his head and looked at her face. She was smiling at him. He got up and stood in front of her while swaying unsteadily and panting for breath.

'Now please try to leave Lily alone for a while, Perry,' she told him. 'The next time you think about coming over here, just go see some other girl.'

Perry backed away until he found himself against the centre table. At that safe distance he watched Molly sit up and sweep several loose strands of hair from her face.

'Lily'll be coming home in a little while,' she told him. 'You'd better go before she comes back and sees you in here.'

Just as she finished, somebody walked up the steps and crossed the porch to the front door. Perry looked around wildly. It was too late for him to leave any other way, so he ran and

85

jumped out the window. Molly was still laughing at him when Jethro walked into the parlour.

'Come on in, Jethro,' she said, beckoning to him. 'I was just sitting here being comfortable. Where've you been all this time? Don't you know how late it is?'

'I thought I heard somebody in here,' he said, puzzled. 'I mean, somebody talking.'

'I was probably talking to myself, Jethro,' she said easily. 'I've been in the habit of doing that more and more lately. Maybe it's just from being alone so much these days.'

'I've been busy downtown,' he said, remembering to explain his absence. 'A fellow down there was telling me he thought maybe Putt might've owned a wheelbarrow, too. He said he saw him pushing one through town once. I've been trying my best to track it down, but it looks like I won't find it. Nobody's willing to come right out and say where it might be.'

'I don't recall ever seeing Putt with a wheelbarrow. He never mentioned it to me, neither.'

'I'm pretty wore out after all that,'· Jethro said in a complaining voice. 'It's a big job looking after an estate these days.'

'Just before you walked in,' she said, speaking in a casual manner, 'I was wondering if you wouldn't want to help Lily and me get a few little things we need at the store. They won't cost much, maybe a few dollars at the most, but they'll be the biggest kind of help. I was sort of figuring in my mind and I'm pretty sure twenty dollars would take care of everything we need.'

She glanced up to see what effect she had had on Jethro. He was shaking his head.

'I was just thinking today that my money wouldn't hold out much longer at the rate it's going. I thought by this time I'd have tracked down a sizeable part of Putt's estate, but so far it don't amount to a hill of beans. All I got for the push cart was five dollars, and I couldn't get but fifty cents for the rubber boots, because they had some big holes in them and the fellow said he'd have to spend a lot of money getting them patched.'

'Half of that belongs to me,' she reminded him.

'Of course it does, Molly. What I'm doing is waiting till I

get the whole estate settled, and then me and you'll share what there is just like you say.'

Molly got up and walked toward the door. 'I need twenty dollars right away, Jethro. I can't wait for it. I need it now.'

She left the parlour and went across the hall to her room. Jethro waited a while before following her. Molly was filling the hypodermic syringe from the gallon jug of vitamin fluid. Jethro watched with mounting interest.

'You look all wore out, Jethro,' she commented while she was putting the cork back into the jug. 'I hate to see anybody in such a rundown shape.'

Jethro, grinning, had already slipped off his overall straps. Then his overalls dropped to the floor and he stepped gingerly out of them and hung them on a chair. Without further delay he stretched out face downward on the bed. Molly quickly reached into his overall pocket and found his money. There was no time in which to inspect the roll thoroughly, so she hastily took the first two greenbacks, which she was sure were tens, and wadded them into the palm of her hand. Then she replaced the roll in his pocket and was on her way to the bed before Jethro raised his head and looked around to see what was delaying her.

'I'm all ready and willing, Molly,' he urged her.

Molly inserted the needle into his flesh and pressed the fluid from the syringe. Jethro made several yelplike yells, but he did not jump and fight as he had the first time she gave him a vitamin shot. He lay with his face pressed against the covering, shaking a little, and waited for her to finish. When it was all over, he got up reluctantly and sat on the edge of the bed.

Molly refilled the syringe, handed it to Jethro, and stretched out across the bed. Jethro plunged the needle into her fleshy rump with such vigour that Molly yelled at the top of her voice. She did not get up, though, and she lay there quivering from the shock while he pressed the fluid through the needle.

'You don't have to act like you're sticking a hog, Jethro. Next time try to be a little gentle with that needle.'

He nodded meekly.

'Now, get your overalls and go on out,' she ordered.

Jethro looked hurt.

'Go on out?'

'That's what I said.'

Jethro picked up his overalls and hung them over his arm. After going as far as the door he stopped and looked back at Molly brushing her hair.

'Where do you aim for me to sleep this time?' he asked solemnly.

'Sleep anywhere you please, just as long as it's not where you oughtn't.'

He waited a while, but Molly did not relent, and he went on down the hall to the kitchen. She could hear him for the next half-hour moving pans and rattling dishes as he searched for something to eat. She heated the curling iron and worked on her hair. She wanted her hair to look as nice as possible when she went downtown to spend the money she had taken from his pocket, and she tried her best to make the curls hold their shape. By the time she had finished, there was a strong odour of scorched hair in the house and her thin tawny-coloured strands were as straight and unsightly as they had ever been. She hurled the curling iron against the wall with all her might.

There was a timid knock on the door. Molly turned around impatiently. Jethro was standing there with his overalls draped over his arm.

'Well?' she said crossly.

'Molly, I've been thinking over what Reverend Bigbee said, and it seems like to me maybe he's right.'

'Right about what?'

'About how it would be a good thing for me and you to get married.'

'And have to put up with you for the rest of my life?'

'It could be worse,' he suggested.

She turned and walked back to the mirror. Jethro watched her brush her hair for several moments.

'Well,' he said disappointedly, 'if you won't, you won't. I still can't find the pallet, though.'

She went to the closet and got two quilts and a pillow. Jethro caught them in his arms when she tossed them in his direction. He gazed at her huge body hopefully while she was walking to the bed.

'Molly, are you downright sure you want me to sleep on a pallet on the floor?'

'If you don't like the pallet, then just sleep on the floor without it.'

She turned out the light and got into bed, leaving him shivering in the dark.

Chapter 10

Iᴛ was mid-afternoon. Inside the house it was hot and humid and Molly was sitting on the back porch where a cooling breeze was blowing from the south and rustling the pawpaw tree in the yard. The mornings in summer were always uncomfortably hot, but there was generally an afternoon breeze that cooled the air and made sitting in the shade the only really pleasant way of waiting for the sun to go down. At that time of year the only perceptible change in the weather came when the summer thunderstorms passed over and left the ground and foliage cool and damp for the rest of the day. The storms could usually be counted on to come at least once a week from June to September, and the farmers in the country around Agricola were always glad to have a soaking rain to help grow their crops. After the early part of September, however, when the cotton bolls opened and were ready to be picked, a heavy rain was always unwelcome and sometimes disastrous. As a rule, though, the thunderstorms stopped when the seasons began to change during the last of August.

Molly had been embroidering a nightgown for Lily since breakfast and, as it was almost completed, she was already thinking about what she could start on next. Lily might surprise her any day by running away with Claude Stevens, and she wanted to have as many nice things ready for her elopement as she possibly could. She had already decided to make Lily a matching dance set and a short crêpe honeymoon jacket that could be worn either in bed or around the house on hot summer mornings.

There had been no knock on the front door, but Molly was

not surprised when she looked up and saw Jamie Denton, who owned the bungalow, walk around the corner of the porch. She had been expecting him for the past several days. Jamie owned a great many houses in town, but he always managed to come for the rent promptly, because he did not believe in allowing the rent to become past due. During all the time she had lived there he had never gone to the front door. He preferred to walk around to the rear of the house and rap on the wooden steps with the end of his pocket-knife as that gave him an opportunity to observe if the tenants were damaging his property in any way. Some tenants had a habit of chopping up back porches for kindling wood and others sometimes dug for fishing worms around the foundations, where the earth was cool and damp, causing the porches to sag or drop to the ground completely.

Jamie could always be expected to come once a month, unless the rent were past due, in which case he generally came almost every day until the rent could be collected. He was a slightly built, medium-sized man in the fifties, who always wore a dusty black felt hat and faded blue work shirts that had been patched and repatched so often that they looked as if they were made of discarded rags. Jamie was one of the wealthiest men in Agricola, however, and besides owning more real estate than anyone else, he had the largest safe deposit box in the bank. He had been married twice, each time to an elderly widow whose husband had left her a considerable amount of property, and by the time his second wife had died and willed her houses to him, Jamie either owned outright or held first mortgages on nearly half the dwellings in town. He received the greater portion of his income from the rental of the sixty or seventy one-room cabins he owned in the Negro quarter. Jamie said the biggest mistake he had made in life was in failing to sell the bungalows and two-storey houses in the other sections of town and investing the money in more cabins in the Negro quarter. He said in addition to having to supply water for white tenants, they demanded that he keep the roof and other parts of the house in repair, which meant actual money out of his pocket, but that Negroes were afraid to call his attention to a leaky roof since they knew by experience that he would not hesitate to make them move out if they complained and then refuse to rent them another house in Agricola. Consequently, the Negroes themselves had to repair the dwellings, and at no expense whatsoever to Jamie.

Molly watched Jamie walk to the steps before he looked up and saw her. He then put his knife back into his pocket.

'Howdy, Mrs. Bowser,' he said, taking off his dusty black hat and fanning his face with it. Without waiting for her to return the greeting, he sat down on the steps. 'Mighty hot today, ain't it?'

'It's not too bad here in the shade of the porch,' she replied pleasantly. 'The breeze feels mighty good, Mr. Denton.'

'It's a puny little old breeze,' he commented deprecatingly, cocking his head to one side and looking up at the sky as though complaining directly to the wind itself. 'A little old breeze like that hardly makes no difference at all. Any old cow switching flies with her tail could stir up more wind than that.' He turned and looked across the porch at Molly. 'A man my age don't have no business being out in the hot summer sun like I'm compelled to be. On top of that I can't stand the heat like I used to could, neither. There ain't nothing I can do about it, though. I have to just get out and go, anyhow. I reckon I'll be making my rounds right up to the time I topple over the brink and die.'

'You know what you ought to do, Mr. Denton?' Molly said provocatively.

'No,' he said, eyeing her with suspicion.

'You ought to retire and take things easy from now on, that's what.' She paused to give the suggestion an opportunity to impress itself upon Jamie's mind. 'If you'd give up all your worries and let an understanding woman take care of you, you'd stretch out your life a long way. You're rich enough with all the property you've got not to have to worry about money matters any more. Now's the time to let a comforting woman look after you, Mr. Denton. You'd be really truly surprised what a loving wife would do for you.'

Jamie was not impressed. He grunted disinterestedly.

'I've already had my share,' he said, shaking his head. 'Besides, I'm too old for that now. It wouldn't benefit me none at all.'

92

'A good comforting woman of about thirty-five would make you feel twenty years younger in no time, Mr. Denton. The only reason I mentioned thirty-five is because at that age a woman appreciates a good man and she wouldn't be running around when she ought to be at home looking after your needs.'

'Nope,' he said, shaking his head determinedly. 'Wouldn't know what to do with a woman at my age. I'm way past that, Mrs. Bowser.'

'Now, Mr. Denton,' she said coyly, 'I'll bet you'd be a regular devil with a woman. I might be afraid to trust myself with you, if I was younger.'

'Nope, I'm too old to bother the women.' He continued to shake his head vigorously. 'Ain't got the will and the way to make up to a woman no more. That's way past my time now. A woman'd be in my way and I wouldn't find no use for her.'

'She could cook your meals for you, Mr. Denton.'

'I'm eating better than I ever did, down at the Busy Bee, and a heap cheaper, too. I'd saved money if I'd done that a long time ago.'

'It would be mighty comforting to have somebody keep you company at home.'

'Ain't home enough to let that bother me. I'm out collecting the rents from sunup to sundown, and then I go to bed and sleep the rest of the time. All a woman'd do would be talk a blue streak, and I get enough of that from the renters.'

'Don't you ever get just a little bit lonesome without a woman in the house, especially at night, Mr. Denton?'

'Nope. All it'd be would be a big added expense for nothing. I'll leave them for the young men to tackle. I've had my day, and I'm glad it's in the past, too.'

Molly was so discouraged that she could not think of anything else to say that might have some effect on Jamie. She snipped off the dangling threads on the embroidered gown and rocked slowly in her chair. She could see Jamie glance at her from the corners of his eyes from time to time, but she pretended to be absorbed in her needlework. She could tell by the way he fidgeted with the brim of his hat that he wanted to change the subject.

'Was mighty sorry to see Putt go,' he said presently. 'I

reckon I knew Putt Bowser the best part of my life, and he was a fine upstanding man if I ever saw one. If he'd lived, he'd have kept his affairs in good shape, too, like he always did when he was alive, because he didn't believe in letting debts run past due.'

She rocked faster, at the same time compressing her lips into a thin straight line. Jamie watched her with darting quick glances.

'Are you talking about the rent, Mr. Denton?' she asked pointedly.

'Well, I was getting around to it, Mrs. Bowser,' he admitted, relieved. 'There's some things in life that has to be taken care of, and I reckon rent's just about the most important and foremost of them all. Of course, I always try to be fair and square about the rent, specially when I'm dealing with widow-women. I ain't a hard man, like some folks try to make out. I just always try to be businesslike, that's all.'

'I need a little time,' she said in a mild and appealing manner, bringing her rocker to a stop and looking directly at Jamie. 'Things happened so sudden that I haven't had time since to more than call my soul my own. That's why I haven't had a chance to give much thought to the rent yet, Mr. Denton.'

'The rent's two months past due now,' he reminded her unhesitatingly. 'I let the first month run past due, because I didn't want to rush around and mention it just when you'd had your sorrow, and now the second month's come around. I couldn't afford to wait much longer, because that ain't the way I like to do business. A month's plenty long enough time to carry the rent for most tenants, and a heap too long for others.'

Molly rocked back and forth, gazing out across the yard at the bushy pawpaw tree. The heavy coarse leaves made a pleasant sound as they rustled in the breeze. She watched their movements until she heard Jamie clear his throat noisily.

'On my way up here from town just a while ago I got to thinking about a few things, Mrs. Bowser.' He paused and glanced to see if Molly were paying attention to him. 'On my way up here I asked myself what a widow-woman with a growing girl the age of Lily could do about paying fifteen dollars a month rent when she didn't have the means. I told myself I didn't want to sound hard-dealing, but just the same I told myself I didn't see how she could keep up the rent. Then on top of that I asked myself if I could lower the rent a little to take care of that, and I said to myself I just couldn't. I ain't overlooked the fact that Putt's brother came to town, but he don't strike me as being the kind of somebody I could count on to pay the rent for you. He just ain't the rent-paying type. Now, what I'm getting at is down to the bedrock plain truth. I sure hate to say it, Mrs. Bowser, because your late husband was a fine upstanding man and he never got behind in his debts, but there ain't nothing that'll take the place of the bedrock plain truth. The fact is, this's a respectable neighbourhood out here in the West End and there ain't nothing else in the world that hurts property values quicker than having a widow-woman under forty, with a growing girl besides, living in a house they don't have the means to pay rent on. Now, I don't want you to go and think I'm singling you out, Mrs. Bowser, because I'd speak the same about the next widow-woman under forty in one of my houses who couldn't meet the rent. The truth is, the first thing you know people start talking, specially the close neighbours, then the talk spreads, and after that there ain't a way in the world to stop it. Before you know it they're saying things that makes the bottom drop clear out from under property values, and then people start moving out of the neighbourhood to another part of town and can't nothing stop them, except lowering the rents to keep the dwellings occupied, and that's one thing I couldn't afford to do. Once you let the rents go down, it takes the devil's own horses to get them back up again. Now, I wouldn't want you to think I ain't all sympathy, Mrs. Bowser, but—'

'Has Lucy Trotter been saying things about me again?'

'I don't know nothing about that, Mrs. Bowser, and I don't want to get mixed up in female squabbling, but just the same there's been some talk around town and it don't take long for it to spread, once it starts. I've seen it go like fire in broomsedge when—'

'I don't see why she keeps on picking on me,' Molly said, wiping her cheeks. 'I'm not bad. I'm just like any other woman. I've always gone to church every chance I had, and I still try to

95

keep from being bad. Lucy Trotter knows that. I wish she'd stop picking on me all the time.'

'I don't want to get mixed up in no spat between females,' he said anxiously. 'Besides, it's too easy to get off the subject. Now, I was thinking what to do about the rent—'

Molly got up and went to the door. When he turned around and looked to see what she was doing, he saw her beckoning to him.

'I've got some wine for you, Mr. Denton,' she said invitingly. 'Come on in the house. A nice glass of wine's just the thing to kill the heat on a day like this.'

Jamie hesitated. He was suspicious of her motives, but he told himself that he had to follow up the rent, no matter where it took him. Molly beckoned to him again, and he got up and followed her into the parlour.

Molly poured two generous portions of wine into the large tumblers. Jamie drank his down without pause and smacked his lips with satisfaction.

'How'd that strike you, Mr. Denton?' she asked gaily as she nudged him with her elbow.

'If I was a drinking man, I'd sure hate to be without that for long,' he replied, chuckling. 'A few more of those and I could be the biggest wino in town.'

She refilled the glasses and took Jamie to the red sofa. He sat down beside her reluctantly.

'I came out here on purely business, Mrs. Bowser, and I've got to get it attended to. Now, as I was saying a while ago. If you'd been married to a man who'd left you the means to live on, it'd be a heap different. But Putt wasn't that kind of man. He gave a little to the church and he spent the rest keeping his bills paid up. Me and you know he didn't own much more than the britches he was buried in. People all over town know that, too, and it's only natural for folks to wonder to themselves how you're going to pay the rent. That's why I've been thinking it'd be a heap better all around if you'd move to another part of town where the rents ain't so high and burdensome. I know you ain't the kind of woman who'd want to see property values get harmed in this neighbourhood. You've got more civic spirit than that.'

Molly poured some more wine.

'I've got some mighty fine dwellings down in the South Side that rent for just half what this here house brings. On top of that the dwellings down there are near about twice the size of this one. And on top of that you wouldn't never have to worry about what folks said about you, because down there there's a different sort of people, and they live and let live. Now, what I've got in mind is a house alongside the railroad that's vacant now and you could move in right away. Besides, if you wanted to do that, I'd be pretty near willing to forget the two months' past due rent on this house.'

'You mean it's down in the Hollow?' she asked.

'Well, some folks call it that,' he admitted.

Molly was silent for a long time before she said anything more.

'People have been mighty nice to me,' she said, sighing, 'and I sure feel grateful. It's a big shock to a woman to lose her husband, and it takes time to get over it. That's why I'd rather stay where I am. I'd hate to uproot myself and move off to a strange part of town. If you'd reduce the rent on this house, I'd always remember you for it, Mr. Denton.'

'Couldn't afford to do that, Mrs. Bowser,' he protested. 'If I was to reduce your rent, others'd hear about it, and they'd say I ought to reduce theirs, too. On top of that there'd be talk attached to it. I've always steered clear of taking anything but the whole rent money itself from womenfolks, and specially widow-women.'

Molly moved closer to Jamie and leaned against his shoulder.

'Nobody in the whole wide world would know about it,' she said intimately. 'It'd be a secret between just me and you, Mr. Denton, and you could come like you always do to collect the rent, only oftener. It'd be company for both of us, Mr. Denton.' She placed her head on his shoulder. 'Two lonely people like us ought to have some company. Don't you feel awfully lonesome at times, Mr. Denton?' She touched his arm with her fingers. 'Huh?'

'Nope, I don't know that I do,' he replied stiffly.

She entwined her fingers with his. Jamie, holding himself erect, looked straight ahead.

97

'Everybody always said I was the loving kind,' she whispered hoarsely. 'I never did think anything was too good for the man I lived with, and I always wanted him to have his way with me. Don't you think a really truly loving woman ought to feel that way, Mr. Denton?'

'Ain't given it much thought, Mrs. Bowser.'

'If you felt you couldn't reduce the rent then, could you leave four or five dollars on the table every time you came?'

Jamie got to his feet, knocking her hands away. He almost stumbled and fell in his haste to get away from her. Molly ran and put her arms around his neck, but he pushed her away and drew up his fists threateningly.

'What's the matter with you?' she demanded angrily.

'I don't want nothing to do with your kind.'

'What other kind are there, for Christ's sake!'

'There's a better kind than yours.'

'The kind that'd take up with an old flea-bag like you?'

'There's plenty of good women in the world.'

'There wouldn't be if you made them all move down to the Hollow so you could keep those houses down there rented.'

'There's a place for women on both sides of town, but down there's where you belong.' He backed toward the door. 'Now, you let me out of here!' he demanded.

Molly drew back her hand to slap his face, but Jamie ducked his head and ran past her to the hall. When she got to the hall, she saw him running across the back porch and down the steps. She was still standing there when Lily came out of her room.

'What's the matter, Mama?' she asked. 'What was all that noise about? Who was here?'

'The son-of-a-bitch!' Molly said, striding to her room. She threw herself across the bed. 'The son-of-a-bitch!'

Lily ran to the window and looked outside. She could see Jamie Denton's slightly stooped figure hurrying across the front yard. When he had passed out of sight, she came back and sat down beside her mother.

'But what happened, Mama?'

'Nothing happened, that's what.' She looked up at Lily. 'There's nothing in the whole wide world more aggravating than an old billy goat who's lost his horns.'

'What did Mr. Denton do?'

'Never mind what he did, honey,' Molly told her as she began to cry. 'You stay away from his kind. They'll ruin a woman quicker than anything else. If they don't perk up when a woman tries to be nice and loving, that's the sign they're the most dangerous kind of man to have around. They'll do you dirt every time. I've never seen it fail yet.'

Chapter 11

MOLLY was stretched out on the bed sipping wine when she heard somebody on the front porch. It had been dark for about half an hour and a cool breeze, following a late afternoon thunderstorm, was blowing through the open window. Lily had just left to go riding with Claude Stevens and Jethro had stayed downtown and missed supper again. She did not expect Jethro to come home that early in the evening, and she decided that Perry Trotter had come again to try to see Lily.

She listened to the rapping for a while before she finally got up, grumbling for being disturbed when she felt so comfortable in bed and put on her green dressing-gown. Before leaving the room she took a hasty glance at herself in the mirror and ran the comb through her hair.

Joe was leaning in the doorway when she walked down the hall. He took a quick draw on the cigarette he was smoking and tossed it behind him into the yard.

'Hello, Molly,' he said right away. 'I hope I didn't break up anything.' They went out into the semi-darkness of the porch. 'I thought I'd drop by and see if you'd be home tonight. Since you don't have a phone, I thought it'd be all right.'

'Sure, it's all right,' she told him, wondering why he had come. She could see his cab standing in the street. The motor was running but the lights had been switched off. 'How've you been lately, Joe?'

'Pretty well. They keep me busy, though. I don't mind the pay, but I don't like this working twelve or fourteen hours to get it.' He sat down on the porch railing. 'There's a lot of people in town these days. That's why I stopped by.'

'What do you mean, Joe?' she asked, curious.

'I remembered talking to you in my cab the other day and I thought you might like to have some company tonight.' He lowered his voice confidentially. 'Of course, I don't know how you're fixed exactly for tonight, but I didn't think it'd do any harm to run out here and find out.'

'Well,' Molly said excitedly, 'I wasn't expecting company tonight, but—'

'That's fine, Molly,' he told her, going to the steps. 'If it's all right with you then, I'll bring him in and make the introduction. He got into town a little while ago and said he was looking for a good time. He looks like the kind who pays his way. He says he sells something or other, and these salesmen always have an expense account, you know.'

'I ought to fix myself up a little first,' she said. 'All I've got on is this old green wrapper. If I'm going to entertain—'

'You look fine just as you are. Don't do a thing.'

Joe ran down the steps and went to the taxi. Molly patted her hair nervously, wishing she had combed it carefully before leaving her room. By then she could see Joe and the strange man coming toward the house. He was short, heavy-set, and appeared to be about forty-five. He was wearing a light grey suit and a white panama hat. His necktie was colourful and arresting, and a handkerchief of the same floral design flowed from his breast pocket.

Molly caught her breath at the sight of his round, almost completely bald head when he took off his hat. She was soon staring open-mouthed at his chubby, innocent-looking face. He grasped her hand and pumped it vigorously.

'Mr. Benny Ballard,' Joe spoke up hastily, 'meet Molly.'

Benny winked and sidled up to her in a loping movement. Then he just stood there grinning. She noticed that the top of his head barely reached to her shoulder.

'How're you, Molly?' he said as he gave her several pats on her broad hips. 'How's the girl?' He sidled closer. 'They always call me Benny,' he told her, winking again.

Molly was so flustered by his attentions that she could not think of anything to say right away.

'I've got a call waiting for me, folks,' Joe said as he backed down the steps.

Benny walked over to the porch swing and gave it a push.

'It's a lot nicer inside,' Molly told him. 'It's always nice and airy in the parlour.'

He followed her inside and tossed his hat on the table beside the tall blue china vase. Molly sat down on the red sofa, being careful to leave plenty of space beside her. Benny unwrapped a cigar and lit it.

'I hope you understand I'm doing Joe a favour,' she said, watching the cigar smoke float around his head. 'If it had been anybody else, I probably wouldn't have considered it for an instant. You understand how it is, don't you?'

'Sure, I do,' he told her with a quick nod.

'Well, now that we know each other better, there's one thing I'd like to know. What do you do for a living?'

Benny sat down beside her, his chubby hand slapping her on the leg.

'I unload farm machinery, Molly. It's a wonderful enterprise. I unload it on the dealers, and they unload it on the farmers. Those poor bastards are at the end of the line and they ain't got a chance with a hole in it to unload on anybody else, so naturally they have to go to work and use it. They'd be damn fools to cultivate weeds with it, so they plant crops and try to make enough money to pay for what's been unloaded on them. The whole sad story is that the smart boys at the head of the line trick the farmers into growing crops and raising stock so they'll have something to eat without having to raise it themselves. I'm a sort of go-between, see? I pass the stuff along from the head of the line to the bottom of it. If we didn't trick the farmers, they'd trick us someway, and have us raising crops while they didn't do a damn thing. Anyway, they'd never raise more than they needed themselves, because they're the laziest bastards in the world to begin with, anyway, and the rest of us poor devils might starve to death. I'm a benefactor to the human race, Molly.' He reached out and slapped her on the leg again. 'That's why I'm called Benny, for short.'

Molly laughed.

'I don't know what Joe told you, Benny,' she said seriously, 'but I'm awfully glad you came to see me tonight.' She shyly fingered the buttons on his coat. 'I like to think I'm the friendly type. I never did think a girl ought to act stand-offish just because she'd never been introduced to a strange man before she met him the first time. Of course, though, I have my rules. I think every girl ought to have her rules, don't you, Benny?'

'Sure,' he said right away. 'A girl without rules hasn't got a chance with a hole in it.'

'I always said a girl ought to be ladylike in public, like out on the street, but when she's in private with a gentleman like we are right now, she ought to change her style so she won't have to be stand-offish. Now, you take us, for instance. If I'd seen you on the street, I'd have looked at you and sized you up, but I wouldn't have gotten familiar with you for anything in the world, because that's one of my rules. But sitting here in the parlour like this is different.'

'Sure, it's different,' he agreed enthusiastically. 'It's as different as one from the other.'

'Another rule I've always had is that there has to be a first time for everything. I always said a girl could get along with any man in the world if she gave him a good time, and there has to be a first time for that. I'd hate to think a gentleman would come to see me and go away without finding out I had that particular rule. Maybe that's why I feel so friendly toward you, Benny. You strike me as being somebody who doesn't have to have all that explained to him. As soon as I saw you I said you're the type who appreciates a good time.'

'That's me, all right,' he said, leaning against her and winking slowly. 'I'm one of the boys.'

Molly fingered his buttons lazily. Her fingers climbed over him from one button to the next, as though she were slowly counting his buttons over and over again.

'So many girls treat men disgracefully,' she told him with a disapproving shake of her head. 'They act like men are just playthings to tease and never stop to think of their feelings at all. A lot of men have had their feelings hurt that way, and that gives women in general a bad reputation.'

'You're damn right!' he said.

'Then there're others who seem to think men ought to be ordered around and made to stop doing this or that. I never was

103

that way at all. I always like to be friendly with a man right from the start, just like I was with you when I saw you out there on the porch the first time. As soon as I got a good look at you, I felt really truly friendly toward you. Some girls would be stand-offish and say they'd have to wait and see if the sun rose Wednesday morning before they'd trust you too far, but my rule is different. I knew you wouldn't have wanted to come to see me at all if you hadn't thought I was going to give you a good time.'

'That's the truth if I ever heard it, Molly,' he said, grinning. 'I'm one of the boys.'

There was a loud knock on the front door. Molly turned her head and listened. Jethro would not be knocking to get in, and neither would Lily. Wondering who it could be, she got up and went into the hall.

Perry Trotter, looking wild-eyed and excited, ran to her. Molly grabbed him by the arm and shook him.

'What do you want, Perry?'

'Is Lily at home?'

'No, Lily's not here.'

'You mean she's not here at all?'

'She's gone out on a date.'

Perry lunged at her, locking his arms around her waist and throwing the weight of his body against her. The unexpected lunge made her lose her balance and she went crashing to the floor. The jarring fall stunned her momentarily. Perry's weight had knocked the breath from her and she found herself unable to push him off. A moment later he was sitting astride her and squeezing her throat with his hands. With a powerful thrust of her body she managed to knock him aside. Before he could get another grip on her throat Benny grabbed him. Molly slowly got to her feet.

'You're hiding her from me—that's what you're doing!' Perry yelled. 'You've been keeping her shut up somewhere so I can't see her!'

'If you ever come back here again I swear to God I'm going straight and tell your mama,' she said, breathing with difficulty. 'I've taken all from you I'm going to stand. Next time I catch you over here, your mama's going to know about it.'

She gave Perry a shove that sent him stumbling out of the hall to the porch. He went away mumbling to himself.

Benny followed Molly back into the parlour, where she immediately picked up the wine jug and filled two tumblers with shaking hands.

'How often do you have him for company?' Benny said.

Molly emptied her glass. 'They all do queer things at his age. It's something you have to expect. That's why I don't want to be too hard on him.'

'Who's that?' Benny whispered, nudging Molly.

Jethro strolled into the parlour, his head bent forward on his neck, and peered questioningly at Benny.

'What do you want, Jethro?' she asked in a cross tone.

Jethro continued to stare at Benny. 'I was fixing to get ready to go to bed, but it looks like the parlour's all took up with strangers. What's he doing here?'

'Go on back downtown for a while, Jethro.' She waved her hands at him. 'Now, go on like I tell you.'

'The poolroom's all closed up for the night.'

'Then go somewhere else. Can't you see I'm entertaining company?'

'I hate that long walk back downtown. I don't see no need for it, anyway. I could just crawl into bed somewhere—'

'No you don't!' she yelled at him as she shoved him toward the door. 'You go somewhere else like I told you!'

Jethro was in the hall by that time and Molly continued shoving and pushing until he was out of the house. She then gave him a final shove that sent him stumbling in the darkness down the front steps. Then she came back into the parlour where Benny was waiting on the sofa.

'Who was that?' he asked with concern.

'Oh, that was just a boarder,' she said indifferently. 'He doesn't pay his rent half the time and I don't feel compelled to furnish him a place to sleep if he won't keep up his rent.'

'He'll have to walk the streets, though, won't he?'

'He'll take care of himself. I never worry about him any more.'

'You sure have some peculiar people around here,' he commented. 'They come in and throw you down and try to choke the life out of you, and then some more come in and argue about wanting to go to sleep on the parlour floor.'

Molly smiled disarmingly as she leaned back against the sofa and began playing with Benny's buttons again. He watched her interestedly for a while as her fingers ran up and down the row of buttons on his shirt and then sat up with a startled look when she giggled. He turned his round flushed face toward her and the sight of it sent her into a spasm of uncontrollable laughter. Soon she was squirming on the sofa and giggling helplessly. Benny tried to hold her still, but by touching her the giggles were intensified. He got a secure grip around her waist and a moment later Molly rolled off the sofa, pulling him with her. He held on tenaciously and found himself rolling across the parlour while her giggling became increasingly loud and convulsive. By that time Molly had lost all control of herself. When they rolled back across the parlour floor, they barely missed striking and upsetting the centre table on which stood the tall blue china vase.

They came to a momentary stop against the wall.

'I guess I do queer things, too,' Benny said to her. 'I never knew I could make anybody giggle like you do, though.'

That sent Molly off into another spasm and they rolled across the floor again and struck the opposite wall with such force that the whole house shook. Benny had hit his head against the wall and he decided he had had enough. Molly's grip around his waist was so secure that he had difficulty in making her release him. He was able to get free of her only after he drew back his fist and poked her in the stomach. That made her double up and giggle louder than ever. Benny watched her with his half-grin, half-frown while he tried to think what he should do. He was still undecided when he saw somebody standing beside him. It was Christine Bigbee.

'I never saw anybody get the giggles that bad before,' he said in amazement, pointing down at Molly. 'She was playing with my buttons and I grabbed her and wrestled her a little, and off she went. She's been giggling her head off ever since, just like that. What do you suppose would happen if I told her some of the funny stories I know?'

As soon as he had spoken he turned and looked at Christine for the first time.

'Who are you?' he asked.

Christine dropped on her knees beside Molly. 'I'm Christine,' she told him. 'Molly! Molly! Are you all right?'

Molly turned over, still giggling, and recognized Christine.

'What are you doing here, Christine?'

'Charles went away, and I thought I'd come over and spend the night. I didn't know you had company, though.'

'That's Benny,' Molly said, pointing upward at him. 'We've been having the best time! He does the funniest things!'

Christine stood up. 'Maybe I'd better go back home, Molly.'

'No, don't do that, Christine.' She clutched at Christine's legs. 'Please don't go away!' Glancing up at Benny, she broke into another spasm of giggling. 'Benny, meet Christine!'

Winking, Benny sidled up to Christine. They were about the same height and he looked less short and stubby with Christine than he had with Molly.

'How're you, Christine?' he said as he gave her a pat on the hips. 'How's the girl?'

Chapter 12

MOLLY was still too weak to walk unaided, but with Benny and Christine's help she went to her room and lay down on the bed. She giggled only once during the next quarter of an hour, and that was merely an involuntary hic and did not aggravate her spasm. Christine was sitting beside her on the bed and holding her hand sympathetically. Benny, slouched in a chair, looked dejected and disconsolate in spite of his habitually cherubic countenance. He had not been spoken to since they came into Molly's room and he had reluctantly come to the conclusion that there was nothing to be gained by staying any longer. He was getting ready to get up and leave when Molly turned over.

'We need some shots, Christine,' she said brightly. 'That'll make us all feel better and pep up the party.'

Christine glanced shyly at Benny.

'He's still here, Molly,' she said in a low voice. 'He's sitting over there in a chair.'

'I owe it to Benny,' Molly told her. 'I want to make up for going into one of my spells and disappointing him. It was a godforsaken shame to let him down like I did. Ask him if he wants a shot, Christine.'

'I couldn't, Molly,' she protested. 'I don't know him well enough to ask him that. He's a stranger to me.'

'He's no stranger—he's just Benny.' She waved her hand in his direction. 'Go on and ask him, Christine. It's all right.'

Benny sat up with revived interest. He could not hear all that was being said, but he had heard enough to realize they were talking about him. A faint smile came to his round chubby face.

'It'd be a godforsaken shame to leave him out,' Molly said. 'I wouldn't want to treat him like that.'

Christine glanced again at Benny. He moved expectantly to the edge of his chair.

'Open the top drawer and get out the you-know-what, Christine, and the bottle's on the floor behind the trunk.'

While Christine was getting the syringe from the dresser drawer and finding the bottle of vitamin fluid, Benny stood up so he could see what she was doing. He looked puzzled as he followed her to the foot of the bed and saw her fill the syringe.

As soon as Christine was ready, Molly turned over on her stomach. Christine immediately plunged the needle into Molly's fleshy rump.

'I'll be damned!' he said, and his mouth fell agape.

When Christine finished, Molly got up and prepared an injection for her. Christine sat down and refused to turn over, but Molly pushed her backward and held her until the needle could be jabbed into her.

Benny whistled. 'What do you know about that!' he said aloud.

As soon as the needle had been withdrawn, Christine hurriedly got up.

'Say!' he exclaimed, grinning uncertainly. 'What in hell are you folks doing?'

'Haven't you ever had one of these shots, Benny?' Molly asked him.

'Me?' He shook his head slowly. 'I never knew about it before. Is it something new?'

Molly motioned to him with her finger. 'Come here, Benny,' she said, smiling at him. 'If you've never had one, you've got a treat coming.'

Shaking his head determinedly, Benny backed away. Molly caught him by the arm and pulled him to the bed. Christine handed Molly the refilled syringe.

'What is that thing?' he said, shaking with fear. 'What does it do to you?'

'It gives you vitamin shots, Benny,' she explained. 'You'll

like it. Once you take a shot from this gun, you'll want more. It puts all kind of pep into you. That's why me and Christine take them all the time.'

'I've been feeling plenty peppy ever since I got here.' He rubbed his hand nervously over his bald head. 'Does it hurt?'

'Of course not.' She pulled him closer. 'It makes you feel so good you don't remember the needle after it's all over. Now, come here, Benny.'

'You girls take it,' he said, trying to get away. 'I don't need a booster. I always have all the pep I can use. Maybe some other time——'

Molly gripped him securely by the belt to prevent him from getting away from her.

'Don't spoil the party, Benny,' she chided him. 'I thought you were one of the boys. Don't you want to have a good time with Christine and me?'

Benny looked at Christine. 'I sure do, but I don't have to have a needle stuck in me——'

'I'm glad to hear you don't want to spoil the party. Now, come here.'

Molly pulled him across the bed. He struggled while they held him flat on his stomach, but after Christine straddled his back he relaxed a little and Molly was able to stick the needle into him. He yelled at the top of his voice when the sharp point pricked him, and it was all Christine and Molly could do to keep him flat upon his stomach. After the fluid had been injected into him, they released him. Benny bounced off the bed and immediately tripped on his trousers, falling flat on his face. He was up again in an instant, and began running around the room rubbing the stinging sensation in his flesh. Molly fell backward on the bed and laughed at him until she shook all over.

Winded and panting, Benny came to the foot of the bed and leaned against it for support.

'What a party!' he said as his usual grinning expression returned to his face. 'Wow!'

'That'll make us all feel a lot better now,' Molly told him. 'As soon as I rest some, I'll feel as chipper as a jaybird on a ginhouse roof.' She motioned toward the door. 'Christine, you take Benny to the parlour and entertain him for a while. I'll be up in no time.'

After they had left, Molly lay quietly for the next half-hour, There had been no sounds from Christine and Benny in the parlour during the time she was resting, and when she got up and put on her green dressing-gown, the house was so silent that she was afraid Christine and Benny had gone off and left her. The parlour door was closed. Molly stood outside in the hall for several minutes listening, but she could not hear even a whisper. Cautiously opening the door a few inches, she looked inside. Christine and Benny were together on the red sofa. They did not see her at the door and, alternatingly feeling angry and curious, she watched them for a long time. Christine's hair had fallen loose and her slippers were scattered on the floor. Her arm was flung over the side of the sofa, and every once in a while she raised her hand and puffed on the cigarette she was smoking. Hurt and unhappy, Molly was about to close the door and leave them alone for a little while longer when somebody noisily banged on the front door. It was so loud that Christine heard it, too, and she sprang to her feet. There was a terrified look on her face. Molly quickly stepped inside and closed the door behind her.

'Oh, my God!' Christine whispered hoarsely when she saw Molly. 'How long have you been in here, Molly?' They heard the noisy rapping again. 'Who's that, Molly? It might be Charles —he may have come back! What'll I do?'

'Maybe you'd better hide somewhere, Christine. Go hide in Lily's closet—but you'd better hurry!'

Benny looked bewildered. He tried to follow Christine, but Molly caught him by the arm and pulled him back.

'Take it easy, Benny,' she whispered.

She waited until Christine had had sufficient time to find the closet before she started to the hall. Benny, his grin subdued, got behind the centre table.

When she opened the door, she was surprised to see Pete Peebles, one of the night policemen. She was relieved to find it was not Reverend Bigbee after all, but she could not think what Pete was doing there. He was a tall, slow-spoken man of about thirty. She had not seen Pete since she left Mrs. Hawkins' boarding-house.

'Hello, there Molly,' he greeted her friendly. 'How are you?'

'Hello, Pete,' she said, trying to think why he had come there at that time of night. 'Is anything wrong?'

'Well,' he replied in his slow drawling voice, 'I don't know, exactly. That's what I came up here to find out about, Molly.'

'Find out about what?'

'Mrs. Trotter, over there, phoned down to the station and said she wanted me to come up here right away and arrest a bunch of folks.'

'Here—in my house?'

'That's right, Molly.' His expression changed and he shook his head sorrowfully. 'I hate to bother you like this, but when a complaint's been made—'

'What kind of complaint, Pete?'

'Disorderly conduct, Molly.'

'Lucy Trotter did that?'

Pete nodded sorrowfully.

'I haven't done a thing to her—I don't even let myself look at Clyde Trotter when he walks past the house, and I don't see why she has to keep picking on me like she does.' Tears filled her eyes. 'I'm not bad—I'm not a bit bad. I'm just like any woman. I try my best to be good. She's got an old grudge against me just because I entertained Clyde a few times when I lived down at Mrs. Hawkins'. But I don't do that any more. I don't even let myself look at Clyde.'

'Maybe so, Molly, but she said—'

'What did she say, Pete?'

'She said she looked out of her window and saw three people misbehaving over here.' Pete looked down at the floor. 'I hate to bother you, Molly, and if it'd been only two people, I wouldn't have, but three people misbehaving is a little unusual, and I've got to follow up that kind of complaint. I'd lose my job in no time if I didn't. You know that, Molly, don't you? It ain't nothing personal.'

'If people would only let me alone, and help me out a little, too, I'd get along all right. But instead of that they're always making trouble. Lucy Trotter's done everything she can think of to run me out of town. She's even trying to get Jamie Denton to put me out of this house. I've got a good mind to go over there right now and—and—'

'Now, wait a minute, Molly,' Pete said. 'That won't help matters none now, and it might make them a lot worse. All I've got to do is come in and look around and make a little investigation, and then I'll go back to the station and leave you alone. I'll be doing my duty, and at the same time I can say I didn't find no disorderly conduct. Mrs. Trotter can't make anything of it on a report like that. Now, can she?'

'No, maybe not,' she agreed. 'Come on in. I'll introduce you to my company.'

They went into the parlour. Benny was pacing the floor, but when he saw the policeman's badge on Pete's shirt, he stopped in his tracks.

'This's my company, Pete,' Molly said. 'It's Benny, from out of town. He's one of the boys.'

'Is this a raid?' Benny asked anxiously of Molly.

Molly shook her head. 'Pete's just investigating,' she assured him.

'What's he investigating?' Benny wanted to know. 'I haven't done anything to be investigated about.'

'Where's the other woman, Molly?' Pete asked matter-of-factly.

'What other woman, Pete?'

'The other one Mrs. Trotter said she saw from her window. She said there was you and a fat bald-headed man and another woman, all jumping up and down on the bed and running around the room.'

'She was seeing double, that's all,' Molly said, dismissing everything with a wave of her hand. 'Wasn't she, Benny?'

Benny nodded quickly and continued to watch Pete suspiciously.

'Benny and I were just having a little friendly fun. You know how it is, Pete, when you go to call on a girl. Everybody likes to have a little friendly fun and play around. There's no law against that, now is there, Pete?'

'There's that disorderly conduct ordinance, and they seem to be able to make that stretch to cover most anything.'

'I've always prided myself on making my conduct strictly

orderly. This is the first time in my life anybody's ever sent the police to complain.'

'Maybe Mrs. Trotter was talking about Lily,' Pete said slowly. 'Where's Lily?'

'Lily's out on a date. She hasn't been here all evening.'

'Well, I don't know who the other woman could've been, then,' he admitted. 'If there ain't nobody else here but you and him, that's all there is to it. I wouldn't want to arrest just a man and a woman for having a good time in their own house, because that'd make me look mighty silly. I'll go back and make out a report and say I investigated but didn't find no disorderly conduct of two women and a man like Mrs. Trotter said she saw through the window.'

He started toward the door. When he got to the hall, he stopped. 'Maybe I ought to take a look around, though.'

'Now, Pete,' Molly said, hurrying to him, 'don't waste your time like that. You can see for yourself nobody's here but Benny and me.' She put her arm through his and walked with him to the porch. 'Sometimes when you have the time, drop in and pay me a call, Pete. I'm here almost every night, and I always did like company. You do that, Pete. Huh?'

'Well,' he said slowly. 'I sure would like to, Molly. I couldn't stay long though. I have to check in at the station every hour.'

'Now, don't forget,' she said, squeezing his arm.

'I won't be apt to,' he told her.

She waited on the porch until he had gone down the steps and disappeared in the darkness. Then she hurried back into the house.

Benny was not in the parlour. She looked for him in her room, and he was not there, either. While she was going toward the kitchen she heard low subdued voices in Lily's room. Opening the door cautiously, she looked inside. The light had not been turned on, but she could see the dim outlines of Benny and Christine.

'I'm scared to death, Molly,' Christine whispered, thoroughly frightened. 'I just know Charles will hear about this now. You know what would happen. What'll I do, Molly?'

'Nothing,' Molly told her confidently. She sat down on the bed with them. 'Pete Peebles didn't find out a thing, and Lucy Trotter didn't know it was you she saw, or she would have mentioned your name to Pete. Besides, we weren't doing anything but taking shots, and I'd like to see Lucy Trotter make something of that. Taking shots is a medical treatment. Everybody has to have medical treatment at some time or another.'

'Are you sure nobody will know about me, Molly? Are you positive that policeman didn't know I was here?'

'Of course. Now, stop worrying, Christine.' She stood up and went toward the door. 'Come on, Benny. Let's go back to the parlour.'

Neither Benny nor Christine made an effort to leave.

'If it's all right with you, Molly,' he spoke up apologetically, 'I'll stay here.' He ran his hand over his bald head with a nervous motion. 'I'd like to stay here with Christine for a while. There's a little something I want to talk to her about.'

Molly walked back to the middle of the room.

'What did you say?'

Benny repeated what he had said.

'You don't mind, do you, Molly?' Christine asked.

Molly was silent. For the first time she realized that Benny and Christine wished to be alone and that she was not wanted. Saying nothing, she left the room and went down the hall. After she had gone to her own room she sat down on the bed and listened to the low muffled voices in Lily's room. Every sound they made hurt a little more and she soon found herself crying. She knew Christine was younger in appearance and much better looking than she, but it was the last thing she wanted to admit. All at once she felt a surge of resentment sweep through her. Benny had come to see her, and Christine had no right to walk in and take him away from her. She put out the light and got into bed and buried her face in the pillows.

It was long after midnight when she was awakened when Lily got into bed with her. She sat up and shook Lily.

'What are you doing here, Lily?'

'Somebody's in my bed, Mama. They wouldn't get out.'

'Are they still there?'

'Who, Mama? Who is it?'

Molly lay down again. 'Never mind. Go to sleep.' She pressed her face against the pillows and began crying again.

She could not go to sleep after that and it was almost dawn when she suddenly sprang out of bed and put on her green dressing-gown. She went down the hall to Lily's room. Benny had dropped off to sleep, but Christine sat up wide awake when Molly entered.

'What's the matter, Molly?' Christine asked.

'You ought to know what the matter is,' Molly replied angrily. 'After all I've done for you, I don't see how you could treat me like this. We've been almost like sisters, up to now.'

'What have I done, Molly?'

'You kept him all to yourself all night, that's what. Benny came here to call on me. Then you came, and this's what's happened. I couldn't sleep a wink. It's a dreadful thing for you to do, Christine. I'll never get over it. We were such good friends, too.'

'But, Molly, you don't understand—'

'What's the use of making excuses?' she said, crying bitterly. 'It's morning now, anyway.'

Benny turned over and looked at them sleepily. Raising himself on his elbow, he gazed at the strange room for a moment, and then turned and looked at Christine and Molly again. An uncertain smile came to his round face.

'Hello,' he said meekly to Molly.

Molly made no reply.

'I've got to hurry,' Christine said, looking through the window at the dawn. 'It's almost broad daylight, and I've just got to get home before anybody's up to see me. I've just got to get there before Mamie does, or she'll know.'

Benny began getting ready, too. He fumbled clumsily with his eyes half closed. Molly said nothing until he and Christine went to the door.

'Where are you going?' she asked Benny pointedly.

Benny glanced at Christine.

'I've got to be leaving, Molly,' he said apologetically, moving closer and closer to the door as though he was afraid she would reach out and stop him. 'Honest, I've just got to go when she does. I wouldn't have a chance with a hole in it if I stayed now. You know how it is, Molly.'

He followed Christine down the hall. Molly stalked behind them sullenly.

'You're just like all the rest of them, God damn you!' she cried resentfully. 'You talk big at the start, and then when something better in skirts comes along, you walk out on me. All you God damn men are just alike! I hope I never see another man as long as I live! I'm through with all of you! Do you hear me, God damn you!'

She watched them with tear-filled eyes until they had gone out of sight and then she slammed the door with all her might and went to her room. She stepped over Jethro's sleeping figure and then stopped and looked down at him. Kicking him savagely, she flung herself across the bed and cried despondently.

Chapter 13

WHEN the bank closed at three o'clock, one of the posting clerks told Claude that his Uncle Frank wanted to see him. While he was walking to his uncle's private office in the rear of the bank building he wondered if he had been found short in his accounts and he tried to think how he had come to make a mistake. Frank Stevens, who was president and principal owner of the Agricola National Bank, rarely spoke to him during business hours and Claude had been called to his office only two or three times during the four years he had worked there.

'Sit down, son,' his uncle said pleasantly when he walked into the office and closed the door behind him. Claude sat down and watched his uncle's face apprehensively. Frank Stevens, who was a large fleshy man in his early sixties and who always wore starched white shirts and well-tailored grey suits, went to the window and stood with his back to the room. Without turning around, he asked Claude how he was getting along with his work. Claude told him that he thought he was getting along all right. 'Like the banking business, Claude?' he asked, suddenly turning around and walking back to his chair at the desk.

'Yes, sir, Uncle Frank,' he said right away.

Frank opened a drawer and took out a box of cigars.

'I suppose you're wondering why I sent for you, aren't you, Claude?' he asked, looking directly at his nephew.

'Yes, sir,' Claude replied uneasily.

'Your accounts are in good shape,' he stated in a matter-of-fact manner. 'It's nothing like that. You've proved to be a valued employee of the bank.'

Claude leaned back in his chair for the first time. He took the cigar his uncle offered him and lit it with steady hands.

'I wanted to speak to you yesterday after the bank closed, but I got tied up with some work and you'd gone for the day by the time I'd finished.' Frank lit his cigar and flipped the match stem at the ash tray on his desk. 'This is a personal matter, son, and I can tell you what's on my mind in a few words. It's about your future, and that's a pretty important matter in a young man's life these days.'

Claude nodded, wondering what was prompting his uncle to discuss his future.

'I've got plans for you, son,' Frank said, looking at Claude. 'Henry Phillips, who helped me to open this bank nearly thirty years ago, wants to retire at the end of this year. His health isn't any too good these days, and he wants to take things easy. I'm getting along in years myself. I'll be sixty-five before I know it. One of these days I'll have to step aside and let a younger man fill my shoes. Of course, I want the bank to remain in the family, and so I'd like to see you move up and take Henry's place. After a few more years of experience you'll be able to take over completely and let me retire. That's the way I'd like to see things work out son. How does it strike you?'

'That sounds awfully good, Uncle Frank,' Claude said enthusiastically. 'When is Mr. Phillips going to retire?'

'I'd like to see you take over Henry's work on January first.'

Claude, completely at ease by then, slid his body deep into the green leather chair and crossed his legs. He had hoped that some day he would be promoted to cashier, but he had never thought the promotion would come so soon.

'That's good news, Uncle Frank,' he said gratefully. 'I've been hoping an opportunity like that would come along sometime.'

Frank Stevens propped his feet on the desk, stuck the cigar into the corner of his mouth, and clasped his hands behind his head. Then, leaning back, he looked at Claude.

'That's fine, son,' he said slowly and deliberately. 'Now, there's only one thing that stands in your way.'

'What's that, Uncle Frank?'

'People don't deposit their money in a bank unless they have confidence in the men who run it.' He paused and puffed on his cigar while he watched Claude. 'I've seen too many banks fail in my lifetime not to know that that's one of the first principles of successful banking. I know men who'll go even further and say it's the foremost principle. Anyway, we've built up a lot of good will in this community and people have confidence in us now. It took thirty years of honest banking practice to get us where we are today, and I don't want to see that lost.'

'That's right, Uncle Frank,' he agreed instantly. 'I wouldn't want to see the bank's reputation hurt, either.'

Frank held his cigar over the ash tray and flicked the ash with his little finger.

'I'm glad to hear you say that, son, because what you do has a lot to do with the bank's future. The solid business people of Agricola will be glad to know that our banking practices won't be changed when Henry and I retire.' He leaned back and clasped his hands behind his head again. 'The one thing that could ruin the bank overnight would be for you to step outside your place and marry Molly Bowser's daughter.' He stopped and watched Claude's expression change. 'I know all about it,' he continued. 'Everybody in town knows about it now. More than that, everybody in town knows that only a few weeks ago your engagement to Bessie Allbright was announced. That would have been an ideal marriage, son, and I want you to think about it and see how soon you can get over this infatuation and marry Bessie. That's the only thing you can do.'

'But, Uncle Frank—' Claude protested.

'Let's look at it another way, son. I feel sorry for Molly Bowser, just as I do for every widow who's left stranded and without means to support herself decently, but my sympathy is wasted in her case. She had an unfortunate beginning in life, and she's been unable to overcome the handicap, but she'll always be what she is now—a woman who cannot and will not adjust herself to the world's conventional way of living. There'll always be women like her, but we do not have to accept them as our social equals. Molly Bowser would sell herself with no more thought than you or I would take a drink of water. And, what's more, she'd sell Lily just as quickly as she'd sell herself. A girl who's been raised on such standards isn't your kind, Claude. I know what you're thinking. You're thinking that you want to marry Lily, and that

Molly Bowser has nothing to do with it. But you're wrong, son. If you married the daughter, you'd be getting Molly Bowser for your mother-in-law. It's common knowledge what she's doing up there on Muscadine Street. Taxi drivers take men up there to be entertained. Besides that, Putt Bowser's brother has moved in with her, and from what I hear about Jethro, there's not much to choose from between him and Molly. She'll have to move away from there before much longer, and there's only one place for her to go. That's down to one of the houses on the South Side. Now, would you still want to argue that you'd want your mother-in-law running a house in the Hollow?'

Claude was silent for a long time. He knew everything his uncle had said was true, and he had been trying to keep it from tormenting his mind ever since he began seeing Lily, but nevertheless he still had no intention of giving up Lily even if it meant losing the opportunity to take his uncle's place in the bank. He leaned forward, resting elbows on his knees, and covered his face with his hands.

'What have you got to say, Claude?' Frank asked.

'I couldn't do that, Uncle Frank,' he said firmly. 'I don't want to marry Bessie Allbright now. That's all over. I've made up my mind about that.'

'You think you want to marry Lily?'

'I know I do.'

'Do you know her last name?'

'It's Purvis, isn't it?' he said uncertainly. 'That was her mother's name before she married Putt Bowser.'

'That was Molly's name all right, but it was her maiden name, because she's never been married before she married Putt Bowser. The question is, what was Lily's father's surname? It wasn't Purvis, because that was her mother's maiden name.'

'I don't know then, if it's not Purvis,' Claude admitted uneasily.

'Neither does anybody else,' Frank told him. 'Not even Molly. Molly was never married to Lily's father, whoever he was.'

'I don't believe that,' Claude said, angered. 'It's not true! It can't be!'

'I know all about it, son,' Frank told him kindly. 'I know the whole sordid history. It all happened a long time ago down in the lower end of the county on the Satterfield farm. There are plenty of others who know the facts, too. I don't believe in holding Lily to account for her mother's sins, but just the same she's lived too long under Molly's influence ever to escape the blight. If Lily were alone in the world, I'd say go ahead and marry her, because in a new environment she'd become a different person, and any woman can overcome a little bit of a past if she wants to. Even Molly herself could become a respectable woman in different surroundings, but who's going to take the trouble to do that for her now? Nobody. The time to have done that was twenty years ago, and I can blame myself, for one, for not having taken her away from that Satterfield farm and the other places she lived. No, she has a grip on Lily now, and sooner or later Lily will follow in her footsteps. You know where that leads as well as I do.'

'It's not their fault,' Claude said. 'Putt Bowser died without leaving them a thing. Just because they're poor—'

'Let's not blame Putt for what Molly is. She was what she is a long time before she married Putt. A man like Putt just doesn't have the strength of character to change a woman like Molly for the better.'

'You've got this all wrong, Uncle Frank. Lily's not like her mother. She's different.'

'Maybe so, son, but why take a chance? Why not play safe and marry a girl like Bessie Allbright who you can be sure isn't going to disgrace you and wreck your banking career? Don't you see the harm Lily could do you? Can't you understand that?'

Claude shook his head. 'No, I don't see it, Uncle Frank,' he said steadfastly. He got up and started toward the door. 'I'm willing to take the chance. It's my life, and if I'm wrong, I'll take the blame.'

He had gone to the door and his hand was on the knob when Frank raised his arm and motioned for him to come back.

'Don't leave yet, son,' he said, frowning to himself. 'Come back and sit down.'

While Claude was walking back to the deep green leather chair, Frank relit his cigar.

'I thought I'd be able to convince you without going any further,' he said, 'but I can see now I won't be able to stop there.

You're as hard to convince as any Stevens once he's made up his mind.'

Neither of them said anything for several moments.

'If what I told you about Molly Bowser makes no impression on you, maybe what I can tell you about Lily will.'

'What do you mean by that?' Claude said, looking up.

'You know Doc Logan, of course.'

'Yes, sir. What about him?'

'Has Lily ever mentioned Doc Logan's name to you?'

Claude shook his head. 'I don't think so.'

'I take it you're acquainted with his reputation in regard to certain girls and young married women in town.'

'I've heard talk,' Claude told him. 'Everybody has. I don't know how true any of it is, though.'

'Did you know Lily has been to his office late at night?'

Claude's lips suddenly felt dry. He wet them with his tongue. 'What are you talking about, Uncle Frank?'

'For the past ten or twelve years Doc Logan has cast a spell over one young woman after another. They always begin by going to him for a headache or some minor ailment, and soon after that first visit they're going back at regular intervals, generally late in the evening, I should say between eleven and twelve. No one has yet been able to prove it, because for some reason the young women won't talk about it, but there's good reason to believe that he gains their favours by giving them drugs or injections, probably narcotic, which produce an effect he desires. Doc Logan's been threatened and investigated time after time, but so far nothing's been proved against him. Just the same I could produce a dozen mothers and fathers, and husbands, too, who would back up every word I've said. Some things become self-evident after they've repeated themselves enough times.'

'Lily wouldn't do that, Uncle Frank,' Claude said with assurance. 'I just know she wouldn't. She's not that kind, Uncle Frank.'

'There's no distinction of kind or anything else. Their names are different, that's all.'

'I don't believe Lily would do that, anyway. I won't believe it.'

'She was in his office from ten-thirty until twelve-fifteen one night last week.'

'How do you know?'

'I have ways of finding out what I want to know.'

'What was she doing there?'

'The usual thing under the circumstances.'

'What do you mean?'

'Just what I said, son.'

'Well, I don't believe it.'

'You will, some day.'

Claude rubbed his face and forehead. He was surprised how cold and damp his skin was. He did not want to believe what his uncle had told him, but the longer he sat there and thought about it the more uncertain he became.

'It can't be true, Uncle Frank,' he said tensely. 'It just can't be!'

'The impossible is always happening in life, son.'

'But Lily wouldn't get mixed up with Doc Logan.'

'But she did.'

'I'm going to ask her!'

'Then be prepared for the worst.'

Claude covered his face with his hands for a moment, and then he jumped up and went to the window. The late afternoon sun was brilliant and blinding, and it reminded him of the first time he had taken Lily riding in the country. He turned away from the window and went back to the other side of the room.

'I don't know what to do now,' Claude said helplessly. 'I didn't think Lily would deceive me.' He began pacing the floor aimlessly. 'I don't know whether to believe you or not. I don't want to believe anybody now. I don't think I could believe anything Lily told me, now.'

'It was a hard thing for me to say, son,' Frank told him. 'I thought I could convince you without saying that, but I didn't. That's why I didn't mention it until last.'

'Somebody ought to run him out of town—somebody ought to shoot him!' Claude said angrily.

'That's not the first time I've heard those very same words. They're getting to sound familiar all over Cherokee County.'

'Isn't there some way to stop him, Uncle Frank?'

'Certainly. Find just one person to testify against him, and the chances are he'll spend considerable time behind bars in some up-to-date cell-block.'

Claude went to the window again and looked out at the setting sun.

'I don't know what I'm going to do,' he said, his back still turned to the room.

'Come here and sit down, son,' Frank said kindly. He waited until Claude was seated in the chair. 'You're excited and upset now. When you have time to think about this thing rationally, you'll make up your mind. I'm not worried about that. When you're ready, tell Lily what you've decided. Don't worry too much about hurting her feelings. She's young yet and there'll be plenty of other men in her life. She'll get over this faster than you think. Don't let it drag out too long, though. The only satisfactory way to handle these things is to make a fast clean break.'

He stopped talking and watched Claude for several moments. Claude stared at the floor.

'Then when that's all done, go back to Bessie Allbright. She might behave a little indifferent at first, but when she knows you want to come back to her, she'll get over that.'

Frank got up and put on his hat and walked toward the door. Claude sat where he was.

'How soon do you think you and Bessie Allbright will be getting married?' he asked.

Claude made no reply.

'Don't wait too long, anyway,' Frank told him. 'You'll want to take a leisurely honeymoon trip somewhere for a few weeks, and then after that it'll take time to get settled in your new home. I'd like to see all of that done and out of the way in plenty of time so you can step in and take Henry Phillips' place the first of the year.'

He waited for Claude to make some reply, but when he saw the expression on his nephew's face, he quickly opened the door and went out.

Chapter 14

JETHRO had become so discouraged that he had not felt like leaving the house for two days. For one thing, he had been unable to find any goods or property left behind by Putt other than the pair of rubber boots and the push cart and, besides that, he had spent the last dime he had brought with him from Woodbine County. Twice he had asked Molly to lend him a dollar, which she brusquely refused to do; and, moreover, realizing that he had no more money left, she was pointedly ignoring his presence. She had not spoken a single word to him for two days and even went so far as to neglect to set a place for him at mealtime. The little that Jethro managed to find to eat was what was left over after she and Lily had finished their meal. Jethro had even lost interest in the trash pile by that time and all he did was to sit hour after hour on the back porch and watch the sparrows flutter among the branches of the pawpaw tree. He hated to think of going back to Woodbine County, because that meant going back to his old job of cleaning the cow barn, slopping the hogs, and chopping stove wood from dawn to dusk seven days a week. He had grown to like city life and he wanted to stay where he could sit in the poolroom and smell the odour of frying fish coming from the café next door.

He had given up all hope of persuading Molly to marry him so he would be provided with meals and shelter, but he had not given up hope of persuading Lily to marry him so he could claim the privilege of staying there. He had tried several times to get Lily alone with him so he could argue with her, but so far she had carefully avoided him.

That night for the first time in almost a week Claude Stevens failed to come to take her riding, and he had noticed that she was restless and worried. She had dressed to go out with Claude and when he still had not come for her at nine o'clock, she came out on the back porch and sat down in one of the rocking chairs. She was gloomily silent for such a long time that Jethro pulled his chair closer to hers and asked what was wrong. The moment he spoke to her, she began to cry. A little later she told him that Claude had failed to come as he had said he would and that she was afraid he had been in an accident.

Jethro waited until she was quiet again and then he moved his chair against hers. Frightened, she caught her breath when he leaned so close he was touching her.

'What are you doing, Uncle Jethro?'

'I've got a little something on my mind I've been aiming to speak to you about, Lily. I've never been married, and I've been thinking it might not be a bad thing to do before it's too late. I wouldn't mind at all being married to the right woman. It might be kind of nice. The one thing I wouldn't want to do is get tied up with a woman who'd irk me all the time, though. I'd want to steer clear of that, no matter what happened.'

'Have you got somebody picked out, Uncle Jethro?'

'I sure have, Lily.'

'Who—Mama?'

'No,' he was quick to say. 'No, not her. I wasn't thinking about her at all. Somehow I've got the feeling I don't think we'd pair off none too well. To tell the truth, I had somebody a heap younger in mind.'

'Who is she, Uncle Jethro?'

'Well, that's just it,' he said nervously. 'That's just exactly what I'm getting around to. Now, I might look like I'm a little too old, but that ain't the fact by a long shot. I feel pretty good at times, and I could hold up my end with no trouble at all. I hate to sound like I'm boasting, but the fact is I'm doggone sure I'd make a good man for you, Lily.'

'Me?' she said, catching her breath in surprise. 'Why, Uncle Jethro, you must be joking!'

He grabbed her roughly. 'No, I ain't, Lily! I ain't joking one whit. I mean exactly that.'

Lily laughed. 'Uncle Jethro, you're nearly three times older

127

than me. Doesn't that sound funny to you? You ought to marry somebody like Mama, who's almost as old as you are. It'd look funny for you to marry somebody only going on seventeen.'

'That wouldn't faze me one whit,' he said, breathing against her face and gripping her tighter. 'I wouldn't mind that none at all.'

'But I would, Uncle Jethro,' she told him. 'It'd be like being married to—to—Mama's husband. I'd feel awfully funny.'

'That ain't got a thing in the world to do with it, Lily. I've gone and made up my mind about that.'

'Well, I haven't,' she told him.

She tried to pull away from Jethro. He drew her from her chair and held her until she was panting for breath.

'I ain't the kind who can be put off,' he told her.

She struggled to free herself from his embrace, but he easily overcame her and pressed his stubbly beard against her tender skin.

'Please stop, Uncle Jethro,' she begged. 'You're hurting me!'

'How about me and you doing that, Lily?'

'I couldn't, Uncle Jethro.'

'How come?' he insisted. 'Ain't I good enough for you?'

'It's not that, Uncle Jethro. It's because you're so much older, for one thing.'

'You don't have to worry about that none, Lily. I don't like to boast now no more than I ever did, but the fact is I'd be as lively for you as the next one to come along.'

'Please stop, Uncle Jethro,' she begged, trying to push him away. 'You're hurting me, and I couldn't marry you.'

'Maybe if you knew more about me, for sure, you'd think different.' He pulled her against him, tearing her dress from her shoulders. 'Maybe you don't know it, but I've been speculating about you ever since the first day I came here. I ain't missed a thing, neither. I sure do like the sights I've seen so far. I ain't had many chances to find out about you, but I've seen enough to know you'd suit me coming and going. My big ambition right now is to have you. I've set my head on that and I ain't easy to budge.'

'You mustn't, Uncle Jethro. You know what Mama'd do if she found out.'

'She wouldn't know about it.' He tore away her dress. 'I ain't one whit interested in your mama now. It's you I'm after.' His grip was so painful she felt tears coming to her eyes. 'I'm all steamed up now, Lily, and I ain't going to be put off no longer.'

'You can find somebody else, Uncle Jethro.'

'There ain't no way to turn my head now.'

'You've got to stop, Uncle Jethro! Please try to find somebody else and let me go!'

'I ain't used to having a woman steam me up and then backtrack away.'

'I didn't mean to do that, Uncle Jethro.'

'You've done it now, and I ain't going to be put off, I tell you.'

Lily slipped out of his arms and ran to the end of the porch. She tried to climb over the railing to escape, but Jethro caught her and pulled her back.

'I'm going to call Mama!' she said desperately. 'If you don't stop, I'll call her!'

'No, you don't!' He clapped his hand over her mouth and held her. 'Now, you treat me right, Lily. You've been fooling around long enough.'

Lily stopped struggling and his tight embrace gradually relaxed. He watched her suspiciously.

'Let's go somewhere else, Uncle Jethro,' she suggested, her manner completely changed.

Jethro looked at her for a moment. 'What do you mean by that?'

'Let's go to another place.'

'Where?'

'Out in the back yard, or some place like that.'

Jethro smiled knowingly. 'You're scared your mama will come out here on the porch?'

She nodded quickly.

'You know what I'll do to you if you try to trick me and run off?'

'I'm not going to run away. I promise, Uncle Jethro.'

He held her arm securely while they were crossing the porch and going down into the yard. Neither spoke while they walked toward the bench under the pawpaw tree. Lily was the first to sit down.

'What about it now, Lily?' he said urgently.

'What do you mean, Uncle Jethro?'

'You know what I mean. What about me and you getting together like we talked about back up there on the porch?'

'But I'm engaged, Uncle Jethro. I'm engaged to Claude.'

'That don't bother me one whit. I ain't interested in that at all. Now, you pay me some mind and quit that thinking up excuses. You come on now and give me what I want before I have to take it away from you. You know I ain't the kind who can be put off.'

Lily was silent for so long that Jethro shook her roughly.

'I'd rather you wait, Uncle Jethro,' she said.

'Wait nothing! I've been told to wait before, and nothing never happened. I can't be fooled that way. Now, how about it, Lily?'

'I want to go in the house first.'

'You know what I'll do to you if you went in there and told your mama?'

'I won't tell her, Uncle Jethro. I promise.'

'How long will you be in there?'

'Not long.'

'Five minutes?'

Lily nodded and carefully moved away from him.

'I'll give you five minutes,' he told her, 'but if you ain't back here by then, I'm coming in there after you.'

Lily got up and backed away from him.

'All right, Uncle Jethro,' she said, trembling.

Jethro watched her run to the porch and go into the house. As soon as she had disappeared from sight he was sorry he had let her go. He got up and watched the light suddenly illuminate her room. He was still afraid Lily would tell Molly, and he expected momentarily to see Molly rush out of the house in search of him. Molly did not appear, however, and after a few minutes he stopped worrying about her. At the end of five minutes Lily did not come back to the yard, though, and he walked slowly toward the house. Just as he reached the window, Lily pulled down the shade and he was unable to see her in the room. He listened carefully but could hear no sounds. By that time it had been almost a quarter of an hour since she had gone into the house, and Jethro began to feel uneasy. The longer he thought about it, the more angry he became. He had made up his mind that he was not going to let Lily get away this time, and he tiptoed across the porch and down the hall to her door. He tried the knob and found that the door was locked.

He stood there for several minutes wondering how he could get into the room without attracting Molly's attention. She was in the front part of the house, but he knew she would come instantly at the first sound of a disturbance. Finally, he could wait no longer and he threw his weight against the door. It flew open, crashing noisily against the wall. Jethro ran inside. Lily, wild-eyed with fright, was huddled on the bed. She was so frightened that she did not even cry out when she saw him coming toward her.

Jethro struck her on the face with his hand, knocking her against the wall. Just as he reached for her, she screamed at the top of her voice.

'God damn you!' he yelled at her, striking her with his fist. 'I'll teach you to trick me!'

Lily cried out again and tried to beat him off with her clenched hands. Jethro hit her again and she was quiet.

'This'll be the last time you try to trick me—you'll know better next time!'

Just then a blow knocked him to the floor. He was dazed, but when he opened his eyes, he recognized Molly standing over him. She had a chair raised over her head. There was another crashing blow together with a faraway sound of splintering wood. He did not know how many times Molly struck him after that, but the next thing he knew he was doubled up in the corner of the room and his head felt numb. He rubbed his eyes in an attempt to see more clearly.

'I've just been waiting for this to happen,' he heard Molly say. 'If I'd had the sense I was born with I'd have run you off the day you set foot in this house.'

Slowly Jethro pulled himself up and sat with his back against the corner. He could see Lily, wild-eyed and tearful, standing behind Molly. Molly picked up the largest piece of the broken chair she could find and advanced on him threateningly.

'She tricked me,' he said bitterly. 'She promised, and then

she wouldn't. I don't believe in letting a woman say one thing and then not do it. Any woman who'd trick a man like that ought to have the daylights beaten out of her.'

'Shut your mouth!' Molly yelled, angered. 'Shut your God damn mouth!'

Jethro watched her cautiously. She was so angry by then that she was trembling.

'I'll know better next time,' Jethro said. 'The next time I won't take no chances. No woman's ever going to trick me again. I'll see to that.'

'There won't be no next time around here,' Molly told him determinedly. 'You're getting out, and getting out in a hurry. I hope to God I never lay eyes on you again as long as I live. Now, get up from there and get out of here!'

Jethro made no attempt to move. He just sat there glaring sullenly at Molly. She saw him turn his head and look at Lily.

'I'd be willing to forget what she done, if she'll go away with me,' he said.

Molly laughed at him.

'I wouldn't hold it against her no more,' he said doggedly.

Molly flung the piece of splintered wood at him. He jerked his head to one side and the rung crashed against the wall.

'I didn't mean no harm, Molly,' he said pleadingly. 'She teased me, and I couldn't help myself. You know how it is when a man gets steamed up over a woman. She'd do that to anybody. You know that yourself. I held off as long as I could, at that. She'll tell you herself I didn't try to do nothing to her before tonight. Now, that goes to prove I didn't mean no harm, don't it Molly? Huh?'

Molly watched him coldly.

'You can't dangle a bone over a dog's head and not expect him to make a grab for it sooner or later. That's exactly what happened to me. I just couldn't hold off no longer and I had to grab for it. Now, you wouldn't beat a dog and turn him out into the street for the rest of his life just because he grabbed for a bone, would you, Molly? Huh?'

'Get up from there and shut your mouth,' Molly ordered. She searched the floor until she found another rung from the chair. 'You're leaving, and I don't want to hear no more of that talk while you're about it, either. Now, get out, Jethro Bowser! Get the hell out of this house!'

Jethro hurriedly got to his feet when he saw Molly swing the piece of wood threateningly. She followed him across the room to the door.

'I sort of hate to be leaving like this when everybody's mad at me,' he said. 'It ain't a friendly way for relations to act.'

'You're no relation of mine, thank God,' she said, unimpressed. 'Get on down the hall.'

Jethro went as far as Molly's bedroom door. He stopped and looked back at her appealingly.

'If I've got to go, I need to take the rest of my clothes with me. It's only another pair of pants and a shirt.'

'Get them and get going,' she ordered.

Jethro ran into the bedroom and opened the closet door. He gathered up the pile of Putt's clothing that had been put there after the funeral. Snatching everything in sight, he backed out of the closet and went to the hall. Molly made prodding motions at him with the stick.

'I reckon you know I ain't got nowhere else in the whole wide world to go except back to Woodbine County, don't you, Molly?' He began moving sideways toward the front door. Lily had left the room and was standing in the hall behind her mother. Jethro took a last longing look at her. 'Maybe some day if you change your mind and send for me, I'll still be alive, Molly. I doubt it, though, because when I get back over there to Woodbine County, they'll work me harder than ever for staying away so long. It's going to be a hard life for me from now on, and I sure would appreciate it if you was ever to change your mind and send for me. Maybe I ain't as good a man as some, but I'd be fair-to-middling. I wouldn't make no trouble for Lily next time, neither. I wouldn't come with that in mind.'

Molly followed him step by step down the hall and to the porch. Jethro went down the steps before he looked back at Molly again.

'Well, so long, folks,' he said sorrowfully, his face drooping and sad-looking. 'God bless you both, for what you is and for what you ain't. I reckon maybe you don't know it, but I feel awfully bad having to part with my relations. I'd be the last one alive to bring it about myself. I reckon you know that.'

'You see to it that you stay away from us,' Molly said, 'and that'll make us feel glad.'

Jethro nodded as he backed away. 'If you ever change your mind, you know where you can find me, anyway. I'll be ready and willing to drop whatever I happen to be doing at the time and hurry right on back over here and help out my kin folks.'

Chapter 15

LILY had stayed in her room all morning, tearfully refusing to come to the kitchen to eat breakfast when Molly called her, and it was early afternoon before she finally got up, took a bath, and dressed. Without saying a word to her mother, she left the house shortly after two o'clock and went downtown to see Claude before the bank closed. She walked up and down in front of the bank for several times before she could find the courage to go inside.

She went straight to the window where Claude usually could be found during banking hours, but the iron grille over the window was closed and he was not there. She looked around the bank frantically. There were four or five customers there at the time and all of them were standing in line in front of the cashier's window. She could see no one else to speak to, so she got into line and waited. It was five minutes before she found herself looking at Henry Phillips through the window. He picked up a stack of greenbacks and dropped them into a drawer.

'What can I do for you, Miss?' she heard him say.

'Where's—where's—Claude?' she asked timidly. 'I mean, Mr. Claude Stevens?'

'Not here today,' he replied brusquely. 'Sorry, Miss.'

Instead of moving away from the window and allowing the customer waiting behind her to step forward, she just stood there and looked helplessly at the elderly cashier.

'Well, Miss?' he said impatiently.

'Where is he?'

'I told you he wasn't here to-day, Miss.' He leaned to one side and beckoned to the customer behind her. 'Sorry, Miss.'

'Are you sure he's not here?' she persisted.

'Very sure, Miss. I'm positive.'

Before she had a chance to try once more to get him to tell her where Claude was, she found herself being firmly pushed aside. As she walked away she could see several of the posting clerks watching her curiously. She wanted to ask one of them if he knew where Claude was, but they were so far away and the enclosure was so forbidding that she felt there was nothing she could do. It was still a few minutes before three o'clock, and she went to the street and waited beside the door. After the bank had closed for the day she looked through the window from time to time hoping to see Claude somewhere inside. One by one the bank employees left the building and by four o'clock she was certain everyone had passed through the door except Claude. She waited another half-hour, but he still did not appear, and then she knew there was nothing she could do after that.

She tried to keep from crying on her way home, and she had to walk faster and faster to keep from bursting into tears on the street. By the time she was within sight of home she was running as fast as she could.

Molly heard her run through the hall and slam the door of her room. By the time she got there, Lily had thrown herself across the bed and was crying as if her heart would break. It was a long time before Molly could quiet her enough to get her to tell what had happened.

'Please tell me all about it, honey,' she said, taking Lily into her arms. 'Is it about Claude Stevens?'

'I can't find him,' Lily wailed tearfully. 'He wasn't at the bank and they wouldn't tell me where he is and I just know something awful's happened. I just know it, Mama!'

'Maybe he went away today on business,' Molly told her. 'Or maybe he took the day off and went fishing. There's a lot of good reasons, honey.'

'But he didn't tell me—and he hasn't been to see me for two whole nights now—and I don't know what I'm going to do!'

'It'll be even nicer when he does come back, honey,' she said consolingly. 'It always seems nicer when a man's been away for a little while.'

'I just can't stand it—I just can't!' She threw herself across the bed, beating it with her fists while tears flowed in streams down her cheeks. Molly tried to take her into her arms again, but Lily was inconsolable. 'I can't stand it another minute, Mama!' she cried. 'I just can't! I can't!'

'But, honey, he'll be back, and then everything'll be all right again. You mustn't let a man upset you like this. It's not good for you. A girl has to control herself at a time like this, or she'll go all to pieces. Now, come here to me and you can stay here and just think about how nice it's going to be when he comes back.'

Lily lay in her mother's arms and sobbed. Molly took off her shoes and dress and wiped the tears from her eyes.

'You just let me take care of you, honey,' she said tenderly. 'I know just how you feel. It's awful to like a man so much it makes you miserable, but it can't be helped. All women feel that way about a man sooner or later. When I was your age, I used to feel just as you do sometimes, but I always got over it before too long. It comes the hardest at your age. You'll outgrow it in time. Now, try not to feel so bad, honey.'

'I don't want to outgrow it and I want to feel bad!'

'But just think how much all this upsets you, honey. Just think of how many other men there are in the world.'

'I don't care how many there are—I want Claude!'

'You'll have him, honey. He'll be back, and you can have him all you want. That's sometimes the nicest part about having a man. You don't realize how much you want him till he goes away and you start missing him.'

'I don't want to miss him—I just want him!'

'I know,' Molly said, stroking her hair. 'I know, honey, I know.'

Lily lay quietly beside her, an occasional sob shaking her body, and held her mother's hand in a tight grip. It was a long time before either of them spoke again. The sun was going down, its last red glow tinting the walls of the room.

'I could never love anybody else as long as I live, Mama,' she said tensely. 'I just couldn't stand anybody else. I'm never going to look at another man as long as I live, either. I wouldn't do that for anything, because I love Claude so much. I'm never going to have a date with Doc Logan again, either. I'll never go down there again. Claude wouldn't want me to. The next time Doc asks me for a date I'm going to tell him I love Claude too much.'

'I wish you'd never gone down there to begin with, but it's better late than never. Don't you ever take up with a doctor again, unless he marries you first. But even then it still wouldn't be a good bargain.'

'I only dated him twice, though.'

'That was still twice too many.'

Molly patted her cheek and got up. She went to the kitchen and brought back the wine jug and two tumblers. She sat down again on the bed beside Lily.

'This'll help,' she said pouring the wine into the tumblers. She handed one to Lily. 'A few glasses of wine'll make you feel a lot better, honey. Drink it down, honey.'

Lily drank two tumblersful and lay down with a sigh. She smiled up at Molly for the first time.

'Claude will come to see me tomorrow night, won't he, Mama? He will, won't he?'

'I should think so.'

'He will. He's just got to. I'll feel so good again when I see him. It'll be just like heaven to be able to touch him again.'

After supper Molly heated the curling iron and worked on her hair. She had bought a bottle of greenish liquid that was guaranteed to prepare the most troublesome hair for curling, but after she had dampened her hair with it and wound a strand around the curling iron, the room was filled with a nauseating odour and the curl finally straightened out just as it always had done. All she could do after that was to stand there and glare at herself in the mirror. Thoroughly disgusted, she hurled the bottle of hair curler out the window and made an ugly face at herself.

'What a life for the female element—it's a godforsaken shame, that's what it is!' She glared at herself until she had to bite her lips to keep from crying with disappointment. 'God damn you!' she said to her own reflection.

After putting on her green dressing-gown she went to the front porch and sat in the swing. Lily had turned on the radio in her room and the slow dreamy dance music floated comfortingly around her in the balmy evening air.

She had been there for about half an hour when she suddenly stopped the swing with a thrust of her foot against the floor. She could hear the sound of somebody walking to the house from the street. Peering intently into the darkness she waited until there was a heavy footfall on the steps. As soon as she stood up she recognized Clyde Trotter, Perry's father. Clyde heard the swing squeak and he came directly to her.

'Hello, Molly,' he said. 'Are you alone?'

'If I wasn't, I'd make room for you, Clyde,' she told him with a laugh. 'It's been quite a while since I saw you the last time. How've you been?'

'Pretty well, Molly. How've you been?'

'Not too bad off, considering,' she told him. 'Come over here and sit down, Clyde. It's a nice time of evening to sit outdoors like this.'

Clyde sat down in the swing, giving it a backward push with his feet. They swung back and forth in silence for a while. Molly was wondering why Clyde had come to see her, because Lucy had told the town that she had given Clyde a final warning and that if she ever found out he had been with Molly again she was going to pack up and leave him. The last time he had called on her was just before she left the boarding-house and married Putt.

'It's good to see you again, Clyde,' she said warmly. 'I don't see much of you any more, except when you walk past the house and I go take a peek at you, even if I did promise myself I wouldn't so much as look at you on Lucy's account.'

'I wouldn't be here now if Lucy hadn't gone to a church auxiliary meeting to-night. It's a risk, but I won't stay long enough for her to catch me over here.'

'Maybe you can stay longer than you thought, Clyde. If Perry can slip out and come over here at night, I don't see why you couldn't, either.'

'Has Perry been doing that?'

'Well, he was here a few times to see Lily.'

'I'll put a stop to that,' he said. 'He's too young to be slipping out at night to see girls.'

Clyde lit a cigarette and flipped the match stem into the yard. Molly gave the swing a shove.

'Are you sure you don't want to stay a little while, like you used to, Clyde?' she asked. 'You know you're always welcome to, when you want to.'

'I'd better not get started coming over here, Molly,' he said regretfully. 'You know how it is. What I came to see you about, exactly, was to find out what you want done about Jethro Bowser.'

'Jethro Bowser?' Molly said in surprise, shoving her foot against the floor and bringing the swing to a stop. 'What about Jethro? He left here two days ago to go back to Woodbine County.'

Clyde scratched his head. 'That's funny,' he said in a puzzled tone. 'He was out at the planing mill yesterday and again to-day asking for a job.'

'The low-down, good-for-nothing son-of-a-bitch!' She took a deep troubled breath. 'I thought I was shed of him for good. But I might have known something like this would happen. He lay around here too lazy to do anything but scratch himself. Then all at once he tried himself out on Lily, and when I caught him at it, I chased him off. And he told me he was going back to Woodbine County! The son-of-a-bitch!'

'Well, he's still right here in town. I saw him in front of the poolroom when I came by there to-night.'

'I've got to do something,' Molly said desperately. 'I don't know no more what than a hog on a ginhouse roof, but something for sure. As sure as the sun rises on Wednesday morning he'll be after Lily again, and the next time he might get her before I can stop him. Next time he'll wait till I'm away from the house and he'll get her as certain as there's a sure hand of God.'

'I didn't give him a job,' Clyde assured her. 'I thought it was strange he wanted to work, because I'd never seen him do any around here, and besides that he's been boasting all over town how he was going to make a comfortable living off of Putt's estate.'

'Run him off if he comes back to the mill again. Stick some dogs after him—do anything to run him off. Maybe if he can't get work anywhere in town he'll go on back to Woodbine County. I hope to God he'll get out of town before he has a chance to ruin Lily's chance to get married. I wouldn't want anything to stall that for anything in the world.'

'Who's Lily going to marry? I hadn't heard about it.'

'The time hasn't exactly been set yet, but if things keep on the way they're going, I wouldn't be surprised to see her and Claude Stevens get married any day now.'

Clyde turned and looked at her. 'You mean Claude Stevens who works in the bank?'

Molly nodded proudly. 'That's right, Clyde.'

'There's something wrong somewhere,' he said, puzzled. 'The Claude Stevens I know, and he works in the bank, too, married Bessie Allbright at Reverend Bigbee's house at three o'clock this afternoon and they left right after that on a honeymoon trip.'

Molly was stunned. She continued looking at Clyde while she shook her head with disbelief that he could be talking about the Claude Stevens she knew.

'What's wrong, Molly?' he said. 'Everybody in town knows about it by now. It's true, too.'

'Good God,' she said weakly. Her whole body slumped downward. 'What's going to happen to Lily now? What's going to become of me?'

'Had Lily been seeing Claude, sure enough?'

Molly nodded listlessly.

'Well, you know how some men are, Molly,' he told her. 'They go with a girl until it looks like nothing on earth can keep them from getting married, and then all of a sudden they'll get another notion and go off and marry a different one. It's always happening, all over. It goes on all the time.'

'I know it does,' she admitted feebly. 'That's the God damn pity of it. Men are as slippery as a ginhouse roof. I didn't think it'd happen to Lily, though. I thought she could hold a man, once she had him. I thought sure Claude Stevens was going to marry her. She did too.' She listened to the music coming down the hall from Lily's room. 'She still thinks so.'

'You mean she doesn't know about Claude and Bessie, either?'

'I'm certain she doesn't. She thinks he went fishing or something and will he here to see her to-morrow night.'

'That is bad,' he said, shaking his head. 'It's real bad.'

'It's a godforsaken shame, that's what it is. Sometimes I wish there wasn't a man alive in the whole wide world. Women always get the dirty end of the stick, no matter what happens, and the men go on doing as they please. I don't see how I can tell Lily about it to-night. That'd be just too much for her. Maybe by to-morrow morning I'll be able to think of some way to say it. It's times like this when I want to shoot a man, and some day I'm going to do it, too. The next time one crosses up Lily, I'll shoot him down just like I would a snake up a tree.'

'She's bound to find it out, and it'd be worse if she heard about it down town.'

'I'll find a way to tell her. She went to pieces this afternoon and it took two hours to quiet her down. If I told her now, she's liable to do anything.'

Clyde got up. 'It looks like all I did was bring you bad news to-night, Molly,' he said apologetically. 'First it was about Jethro, and now it's about Claude Stevens marrying Bessie Allbright.' Molly walked to the steps with him. 'Lucy'll be getting home pretty soon now and I wouldn't want to be caught over here. I'd better hurry, Molly.'

Molly dabbed at her eyes with her handkerchief. 'The bottom's dropped clear out from under me,' she said, bowing her head. 'I don't know what I'd do if I didn't know you'd always give me a helping hand when I needed it, Clyde. Of course, I wouldn't call on you for help unless I really needed it, but it's good to know I could if I wanted to.'

'That's right, Molly,' he said uneasily. 'You just let me know if there's anything I can do.'

'I could use about ten dollars right now,' she said quickly.

Clyde dug into his pocket and handed her several greenbacks. Then he hurried across the yard.

'If I ever get settled right,' she called after him, 'you'll have the big shiny key to my front door, Clyde.'

Chapter 16

I⊤ was late afternoon when Molly looked out the window and saw a large, new two-tone sedan stop in front of the house. It was a more expensive-looking automobile than she had ever seen before in Agricola and she had no idea what it could be doing in front of her house until she recognized Benny Ballard. He stepped to the ground and carefully whisked the lapels of his blue suit with his hands. Then he placed his straw hat at an angle on his round bald head and started toward the house.

Molly was waiting, eager and expectant, when he bounded up the steps two at a time and crossed the porch. As soon as he saw Molly standing in the doorway he took off his hat and nervously ran his hand over his shiny head. His ingratiating grin, as innocent-looking as ever, fixed itself upon his flushed face.

'How's the girl, Molly?' he said, sidling up to her in the familiar manner which she remembered so well and patting her lightly on the hips. 'It's sure good to see you again, Molly. You remember me, don't you? Benny Ballard, the bastardly unloader? Heard any farmers cussing me out lately?'

'I wouldn't be apt to disremember you this soon, Benny,' she said pleasantly. 'How've you been lately?'

He gave her another familiar pat and winked broadly. 'Ain't complained yet. Everything's sevens and elevens.'

They went into the parlour and Benny dropped his new stiff-brim straw on the centre table and began unwrapping a cigar. Molly sat down on the red sofa and watched him with increasing anticipation.

'I want to tell you right away, Benny,' she said demurely,

143

'that I owe it to you to make up for the scandalous way I let you down the last time you came to see me. I'll try to keep a grip on myself this time so nothing like that'll happen again. It was all my fault and I don't hold any hard feelings against you at all.'

'Forget it, Molly,' he said with a flourish of his hand.

'I had no idea you'd be back in town again this soon,' she went on. 'I thought you only came two or three times a year.'

'This's an extra trip. It's a little something I worked up the last time I was in town.'

He lit the cigar and looked at his watch. Molly noticed that his hands were shaking slightly and that he looked more serious than usual.

'How long will you be here this time, Benny?' she asked brightly. She shook her finger at him with a stern gesture. 'Now, you be sure and stay long enough for me to give you a good time. I'm not going to be the one to let history repeat itself.'

Benny cleared his throat and looked nervously out the window. He did not answer her and the grin on his face was gradually disappearing. Presently he came to the sofa and sat down on the far end. Molly looked at him strangely.

'Is something wrong, Benny?' she asked, wondering. 'You don't seem like your old self.'

Benny glanced at his watch again.

'No,' he said with a jerky motion of his head. 'No, there's nothing wrong, that I know of.' He puffed nervously on the cigar. 'I hope nothing's wrong, anyway.'

Molly wondered why he was acting so strangely and she tried to recall if she had said anything that might have displeased him.

'It's getting late,' he said, turning and looking out the window. 'It's after five already.'

'What's that got to do with it, Benny?' she asked, distressed. 'Aren't you going to stay all night?'

He turned to her with a frightened glance. She could see a solemn frown on his face.

'I might as well tell you now, Molly,' he said, speaking rapidly, 'because you'll find out in a few minutes, anyway.' He moved closer and lowered his voice. 'Christine's going to meet me here.

She said she'd be here at five.' He glanced at his watch once more. 'It's already a quarter-past five. Do you think something might have happened?'

'Couldn't you wait till after dark?' she said coolly, unable to hide her disappointment. 'Why do you want Christine Bigbee again, anyway? What's wrong with me?'

'You don't understand, Molly. Christine's going away with me. We're leaving town together as soon as she gets here.'

Molly was stunned. She looked at Benny incredulously.

'You and Christine?' she said. 'Eloping?'

Benny nodded.

'Running away together—you and her?'

He moved his head up and down again.

'But what will Reverend Bigbee say?'

'I don't know.'

'But won't he try to find you and Christine and make her come back?'

'By the time he finds out about it we'll be a hundred miles from here. He won't be able to stop us then.'

'Are you going to get married?'

'Not right away. We couldn't do that till Christine gets a divorce. That'll take time.'

'Where are you going when you leave here?'

'I don't know exactly. But we'll tuck ourselves away in a little corner somewhere.'

Molly sighed. 'Well,' she said, 'that's certainly a surprise to me. I didn't know anything like that was afoot. Of course, I noticed how you and Christine made up to each other that night, but I didn't think it amounted to anything more than a good time. When did Christine say she'd go away with you?'

'That same night. We got it all planned before she left the next morning. That's why I had to leave when she did, Molly.'

Molly looked down at her hands while she fingered a seam of her skirt. She saw from the corners of her eyes that he was glancing at the time again.

'It makes me feel awfully bad,' she said sorrowfully. 'I've been hoping and praying somebody would come along and want to marry me, but every time I get close to it, it looks like something happens to spoil my chances. Sometimes I think I've got a curse on me. I don't know why that is, either, unless it's because the good Lord made two kinds of women, one kind that men take to and marry, and the other kind, like me, who always get left out in the end. It makes my blood boil to see some women get themselves a man, when most of them can't give a man nowhere as good a time as I can. I wouldn't say that if I didn't know what I was talking about, either. There's no justice in that—it's just that godforsaken curse I've got on me. Everything I touch goes sour. I try to make a living, but I can't get a job. I try to get Lily married off so she won't have the sorrow in life that I've had, and another woman comes along and edges her out. I try to find myself a good man, and either he won't leave his wife for me, or else he goes and finds himself another woman. Sometimes I think it's all because I didn't have the right kind of start in life, and now I can't get out of the rut. If my parents hadn't died, and if it hadn't been for those God damn Satterfields, I'd have had a better chance. Something went wrong when that happened —losing my folks and going to live with those God damn Satterfields. God Himself knows it ruined me. I hope there're not many women like me in the world, and I feel sorry for every last one of them that there is.'

Benny got up and walked back and forth, stooping and glancing worriedly at the street each time he passed the window.

'I don't want you to have any hard feelings against Christine and me,' he said anxiously. 'It's just that we hit it off like sevens and elevens from the start, and that's something a man can't ignore. It's a great feeling to find yourself being a fool about a girl like Christine, and if I didn't go ahead and take her while I can, I'd regret it all the rest of my life.'

'That's all right, Benny,' she said as she wiped tears from her cheeks. 'If you'd taken up with me instead of with Christine, something'd have gone wrong for sure. I just know it would. The curse I've got on me would've messed things up. It looks like I can draw men like molasses, but as soon as they see somebody better looking, off they go. It's been the same sad story all along. I reckon the only thing for me to do is take heed and put it to some use. I've got to support myself some way, and God Himself knows it's the only way I can do it. Jamie Denton knew what he was talking about when he said the thing for me to do was to go down to the South Side. I've tried every way I could think of to stay away from there, but I can't hold out against it and starve at the same time.'

Benny stopped and bent over in order to see better through the window. His face lighted up and his customary broad grin returned to his florid face.

'Here she comes now, Molly!' he called out excitedly. 'She's running across the yard!'

Molly remained seated on the sofa and dried her tears while Benny was going to meet Christine at the door. Molly heard her utter a breathless cry when Benny put his arms around her. They remained in the hall for several minutes before Benny brought her into the parlour.

The two women looked at one another without a word being spoken. Christine was dressed in a soft grey suit and a small flowered hat that made her look five years younger. Her eyes sparkled brightly. Enviously, Molly said to herself that Christine could almost pass for a schoolgirl.

Benny, who still had his arm around her waist, drew Christine across the parlour.

'Molly knows all about it, Christine,' he said solicitously. 'I've just told her everything. She knows all about it now.'

'I'm scared to death, Molly,' Christine said, leaving Benny and coming to the sofa. She sat down tensely. 'I'm so afraid something'll happen I don't know what to do. I feel like I'm breaking out of jail and knowing they'll start looking for me any minute. Do you think I'm doing the right thing, Molly? Wouldn't you do it if you were in my place?'

'Where's Reverend Bigbee?' Molly asked.

'He's still at home, I suppose. I slipped away while he was busy in the library. I hated to go away like that, but I didn't know any other way. I left a note pinned on the pillow. He'll find it when he starts looking for me. I never did feel that I was really married to Charles. Maybe it was because I just wasn't made to be a minister's wife. That's why I don't feel that I'm doing such a terribly bad thing, Molly. Don't you think it's all right under the circumstances? Wouldn't any woman do it if she had the courage?'

'We'd better be going, Christine,' Benny said anxiously. 'We don't want to get caught before we can leave town.'

'We'll have to wait till dark, Benny. If we drove through town now, somebody would be sure to recognize me. It'll be dark in just a little while. It's almost six now.'

'But suppose he finds the note right away and starts looking for you?' He looked at his watch and then looked out the window at the late afternoon light. 'I don't want to get caught here to-night,' he told her. 'That'd be a shame. Can't we leave right now, Christine?'

Christine looked out the window.

'Let's wait just a little longer, Benny,' she begged. 'It'll be completely dark soon, and then we can be sure nobody will see us.'

'I wish it was me who was eloping,' Molly said wistfully. 'God Himself knows how much I've wanted to find somebody who'd take me off like this. I don't know what I'm going to do when you're gone, Christine. You're the only friend I've got, and now you're leaving.'

'Now, Molly,' Christine said sympathetically, 'don't feel so bad. You wouldn't want me to give up a chance to leave, would you?'

'No, I guess not,' she admitted. 'There won't be anybody I can visit like I used to you, though. We used to have such good times together, Christine, just me and you.' She began to weep. 'We'd give each other shots with the gun and talk about Reverend Bigbee and smoke cigarettes and have such a good time. All that's over now. You won't be here after this, and I'll be all alone.'

Christine reached over and held Molly's hand.

'You'll find somebody, Molly. One of these days a man will come along, just like Benny did, and then it'll be different.'

'That's right, Molly,' Benny spoke up. 'I wouldn't be surprised if you had a chance to pick and choose.'

'Oh, shut up!' Molly cried unhappily. 'I thought you liked me once, but then when Christine came along you dropped me like a rock on a ginhouse roof. I don't have faith in men any more. They're always on the lookout for somebody younger or better-looking. Don't try to tell me different, because I know!'

Christine and Benny glanced uneasily at each other. Molly

was crying and dabbing awkwardly at her tears with her handkerchief.

'Let's go, Christine,' he urged. 'It's dark enough now. Come on!'

Christine got up and looked out the window.

'Are you sure, Benny?' she asked him.

He took her by the arm and started toward the door. Christine stopped and looked back at Molly weeping on the sofa. Running to her, she threw her arms around Molly and hugged her tightly.

'Please don't think too hard of me, Molly,' she begged. 'It's my only chance to get away while I'm still young enough—I might not have another chance. I've just got to go! You understand, don't you?'

Molly patted her shoulder and nodded briefly.

'Good-bye, Christine,' she murmured tearfully. 'God bless you.'

Christine buried her face against Molly for a short moment and then, getting hastily to her feet, ran to Benny. They walked hurriedly out of the parlour without looking back.

Molly could hear them going down the front steps. Soon after that the door slammed, the engine started, and the car roared away into the night. She sat on the sofa, holding back her sobs as best she could, and thought about Christine and Benny and wished they had taken her with them. She was no longer angry, but it did hurt her to know that Benny had come back for Christine instead of for her. Drying her tears, she got up and turned on the hall light.

Lily was still locked in her room, where she had been all day since Molly told her at breakfast about Claude and Bessie Allbright. Molly knocked on her door and called her several times, but Lily would not answer, and all she could hear was an occasional sob that was partly muffled by the pillow.

Molly prepared something to eat and finished as quickly as she could. While she was washing and drying the dishes, she heard somebody tiptoe across the back porch. She waited and listened, and then she found herself looking at Jethro's dimly outlined face through the window. Her first thought was to find something she could hurl at him, but the longer Jethro stared at her the less inclined she became to drive him away. Her hands trembled and she was surprised to feel a yearning for him.

149

Putting aside the dishes, she went outside to the dark porch. Jethro immediately backed away and stood at the railing ready to leap to the ground.

As her eyes became accustomed to the darkness, she watched him silently. Jethro was nervous and unable to stand still. He leaned against one of the posts.

'What do you want here, Jethro?' she said after a while.

'Well, now, Molly,' he began hesitantly, 'that's a pretty big question to answer right off the bat. I wouldn't know exactly right where to begin. Anyhow, I had a feeling—'

Molly went to the rocking-chair and sat down. Jethro watched her hopefully.

'Where've you been since you left here?' she asked.

'Just here and there and nowhere in particular, Molly.'

'Why didn't you go back to Woodbine County?'

'I just couldn't bring myself around to do that, Molly. I sure like it over here a heap better.'

Molly was silent for a while. She rocked as fast as she could.

'I never felt so godforsaken sad and lonely in my whole life, Jethro,' she said presently. She brought the chair to a stop. 'I don't know how you feel, but that's something a woman can hardly stand. It does queer things to you. It makes me want to stop living.'

She began rocking the chair gently.

'When lonesomeness gets so bad you can't stand it, you're willing to do anything in God's world to stop it. I know, because I've had it so often that now when I feel it creeping up on me, I'd rather be dead than have to stand it again. There's a lot of things a human being can stand, but lonesomeness is not one of them. Lonesomeness is the worst feeling there is. It's the one time when you'd rather be dead than alive.'

Jethro began to edge across the porch toward Molly. He came part way and stopped to see if she had noticed him. She said nothing and, taking heart, he moved closer and closer until he was standing against the railing in front of her. He could have reached out and touched her if he had had the courage.

'I don't know what to do,' Molly said with a helpless gesture of her hands. 'I can't stand this lonesomeness any longer, and if I thought I could trust you to leave Lily alone—'

'Oh, I'll promise that ten times over,' he assured her without a moment's hesitation. 'That's one promise I can make for sure. There wouldn't be no need to bother her, anyhow, if me and you—'

'God damn you men!' she cried out, putting her hands over her face. 'What a life for the female element! God damn all you men!'

Jethro watched her anxiously. 'Molly, I'll sure-God promise what I said just now. I mean every word of it, too.'

Molly's hands dropped to her lap as tears began running down her cheeks. After several moments she got up, motioning for Jethro to follow her. When they were in the kitchen, she stopped at the table and dried her tears on the hem of her skirt. Then she turned to Jethro, a smile breaking out on her face.

'What do you want to eat, Jethro?' she asked with a sob. 'I can fry you some hog sausage and heat up some beans. Would you like that, Jethro?'

'I sure would, Molly,' he told her gratefully. 'I've been wanting a real womanly meal so bad I didn't know what to do.'

Chapter 17

'Now who is that?' Molly said in an exasperated tone of voice.

She put down the frying-pan she had been scouring and, with arms akimbo, scowled darkly at Jethro as if blaming him for the intrusion. Jethro meekly shook his head. He had finished eating the sausage and warmed-over beans, and he was still sitting at the kitchen table. He cocked his head and listened to the disturbance in the hall. Molly drew a deep resigned breath and waited. Somebody was noisily clomping into and out of the parlour, and after that they heard the same jarring footsteps in Molly's bedroom.

'Living in this place is worse than trying to have some privacy on a ginhouse roof,' she said. 'I've never seen anything like it. You never know from one minute to the next who's coming or what for. I reckon the only thing to do is put some locks on the doors, but that'd be sure to make a lot of disagreeable enemies.'

The clomping footsteps, resounding in the hall again, were coming closer. Jethro shoved his chair around so he could face the doorway. Molly's left hand swept several loose strands of hair from her face.

At that moment the wild-eyed and agitated face of Reverend Bigbee appeared in the doorway. The lines in his long face were deeper and sharper than Molly had ever seen them before. His loose skin was ash-coloured.

'Oh, my God!' Molly cried out, startled by his appearance.

She swayed unsteadily for a moment and then reached out

and grasped the back of a chair for support. Holding to the chair, she moved her heavy body until she was in a position to sit down.

Reverend Bigbee took several steps forward, at the same time craning his neck and peering suspiciously around the kitchen. Then he turned, frowning, to Molly.

'Where is she?' he hoarsely demanded.

Molly's lips parted but she uttered no sound.

'Where is she?' he repeated in the same hoarse voice.

She shook her head as she watched him fearfully.

Reverend Bigbee turned to Jethro with a threatening movement of his tall body. Jethro hastily got to his feet and, in a stumbling motion, knocked over the chair.

'Have you seen her?' he demanded of Jethro.

Awkwardly uprighting the chair, Jethro shook his head.

After glaring suspiciously first at Jethro and then at Molly, he turned and strode out of the kitchen and went to the hall. When he saw the door to Lily's room, he stopped and knocked loudly. There was no reply, and he flung the door open and went inside. After a hasty look at the room he began searching the closet. Lily was so surprised to see Reverend Bigbee that she sat up and stopped crying. He got down on his knees and looked under the bed.

'Has she been here?' he asked her.

Lily, still wondering what he was doing in her room, shook her head.

'Have you seen Mrs. Bigbee, Lily?'

'No, sir,' she replied.

'Are you sure, Lily?'

'Yes, sir.'

He flung the closet door open and once more searched it carefully before leaving and going back to the kitchen.

Molly and Jethro, who had watched Reverend Bigbee search Lily's room, stepped back out of his way. Drawing a chair to the kitchen table, he sat down with a groan. His black hair was rumpled and uncombed and he was wearing only his coat over his undershirt.

With a nervous motion he put his hand into his pocket and drew out a crumpled sheet of paper.

'I found this on my pillow,' he said accusingly to Molly. 'Christine left it there.' He squeezed the paper in the palm of his hand. The unruly lock of black hair fell further over his forehead. 'She's gone away—left me,' he said in a voice of anguish. His shoulders drooped pathetically and the loose ash-coloured skin sagged from his chin. 'I don't understand it—I was always a good husband to her. Why does a woman do a thing like that—what possesses her?'

He gazed forlornly at Molly.

'I did my best to make her contented, but for some reason she was never satisfied. She liked worldly things more than the simple things of life. She wanted the latest styles in clothes, she wanted to go to the movies, she wanted to listen to dance music on the radio—she wanted to do everything I disapprove of. She even wanted me to let her smoke cigarettes when we were alone, and in order to get her way she tried to make me smoke them, but of course I wouldn't. Time after time I had to make her change her clothes, because some of the garments she wanted to wear were disgraceful. I thought after ten years I had convinced her of everything that was good for her. And now she's gone and done this. I don't know what I'm going to do. It's an awful blow to a man in my position to have his wife run away.'

Lily came to the door to listen to what Reverend Bigbee was saying.

'If I only knew where she went,' he said with an appealing look at Molly, 'if I only knew. I'd gladly bring her back and forgive her. I wouldn't mind doing that, because I could pray for her and make her feel sorry for what she's done. But I don't know which way to turn. She's run away like a spoiled child.' He leaned forward and looked searchingly at Molly. 'Do you have any idea where she went, Mrs. Bowser?'

Molly shook her head. 'She didn't say where she was going, exactly.'

Reverend Bigbee leaped to his feet. 'That means you've seen her!' He stood in front of Molly. 'Where is she, Mrs. Bowser? Where did she go? When did she leave?'

'I don't know, Reverend Bigbee,' she told him, shaking her head. 'She didn't tell me. That's the honest truth, Reverend Bigbee.'

He looked at her harshly. 'God wants you to tell me the truth, Mrs. Bowser.' He came closer. 'Was she alone, Mrs. Bowser? Was anybody with her?'

'Well, yes, I seem to remember somebody with her,' she said, feeling as if some compelling force were putting words into her mouth. 'Come to think of it, there was.'

'Who? Who was it?'

'A man.'

He started to raise his hand to his face, but it fell limply against his thigh.

'She went away with a man?' he said, shaking his head with disbelief.

She nodded.

'I can't believe it—who was he?'

'He's a salesman—a very high-class gentleman. I'd been introduced to him before. I was proud to know him.'

'Oh, Lord!' he muttered. 'What's his name?'

'Mr. Benny Ballard.'

'Where did he come from? How did Christine get to know him? When did she meet him?'

'He came to town selling farm machinery. Benny's a very high-class gentleman. You don't run across many fine men like him these days.'

'God in His heaven have mercy,' he said to himself as he sat down and ran his fingers through his hair.

'As long as Christine was eloping,' Molly said, 'it was a lot better for her to run away with Benny Ballard than with a lot of others I could name.'

'Do you know where they went, Mrs. Bowser?' he asked in a weary voice.

'They wouldn't say, Reverend Bigbee. They wouldn't tell me a thing about their future plans. All they'd say was that they were going where nobody could find them. I wouldn't know where to begin looking for them.'

'This is terrible,' he said, covering his face with his hands. 'It's a lot worse now than I'd thought in the beginning. It's a disgrace. I'm ruined. No congregation wants a pastor whose wife ran away to live in sin with another man. I've come to the end. I can't go on.'

Molly listened to his agonized groans and tried to think of something she could say that would cheer him up. He sat there with his head bowed and his face covered with his hands.

'You oughtn't to blame Christine too much, Reverend Bigbee. It happens all the time. A lot of women get dissatisfied and think the only thing to do is run away with some man. A lot of them are just as spirited as Christine, and they think they ought to go while they have a chance. They figure if it doesn't work out, they can always come back.'

'But I always did what I thought was good for her.'

'Only a woman knows what's good for her, and she'll let you know what it is. If you'd listened to Christine and let her have her way a little, this wouldn't have happened. She tried hard to tell you. She told me so herself.'

He waved his hand, silently pleading with her to stop. Then he got up and paced the floor.

'I don't know what you're talking about. I don't know what you mean.' He walked back and forth across the kitchen several times. 'All I know is I'm ruined—ruined for life. I'm a disgraced man. I could never hold my head up in Agricola again if I lived to be a hundred years old. The shame is too great. The finger of scorn would be forever pointed at me. I've reached the end of existence. Good Mrs. Trotter warned me in so many words, time after time, that Christine was not suited to be a minister's wife— I should have listened to Mrs. Trotter before I married Christine. Mrs. Trotter would have made a good minister's wife. But it's all too late now—it's all too late. I've come to the end.'

He continued through the doorway when he crossed the kitchen and they heard him wandering through the other rooms in the front of the house. Molly shook her head sadly to herself.

All three of them listened to the aimless wandering of Reverend Bigbee from one room to the next.

'I feel sorry for him,' Molly said, sighing, 'but there's nothing I can do. He brought it on himself, and he knows it. That ought to be a lesson to him, though. Maybe his next wife, if he ever has one, will benefit by it.'

'What's he going to do, Mama?' Lily said. 'Is he going to stay here and walk the floor like that all night?'

'What can you do for a man like him?' Molly replied. 'You

can't console him, because you can't get close enough to him to take his mind off his troubles. What else is there to do? Nothing!'

'I hate to see him so upset, Mama. I don't like to see anybody feel as bad as he does, and not do anything to help him.'

Molly shook a finger at Lily. 'You stay away from him, do you hear me? This is one time when I don't want to see you make a move. I'm not going to stand here and see you get tangled up with Reverend Bigbee. There's a limit, and he's it.'

'But if I only talked to him, Mama, it might help.'

'No-sirree-bob!' she said flatly, shaking her finger at Lily again.

There was a heavy thud in one of the rooms that jarred the house. Jethro stood up and looked around.

'What was that noise, Jethro?' Molly said.

'It sounded like something heavy fell,' he said.

'Where did the sound come from?'

'Somewhere up there,' he said, pointing up the hallway.

The three of them left the kitchen and walked cautiously toward the front part of the house. Molly was the first to look into her room. She screamed.

Reverend Bigbee was sprawled on the bare floor and a vivid stain was spreading over the pine boards. He still clutched a jagged piece of broken wine tumbler in his right hand. He had removed his coat and thrown it across the bed before slashing his arm with the glass.

'Lily, hurry over to the Trotters' and phone for the doctor,' Molly said, shoving her toward the front door. 'Hurry, Lily!'

'Do you want me to call Doc Logan?'

'No. Call anybody else but him. I don't want him around here if I can help it.'

She pushed Lily out of the house and went back to her room. As she and Jethro bent over Reverend Bigbee she could see his chest move as he breathed. His eyes were open, but he did not recognize her. She got a towel from the washstand and she and Jethro twisted it around his arm above the elbow.

'Reverend Bigbee—' she said to him. 'Reverend Bigbee, are you all right?'

He made no reply. Jethro tightened the towel around his arm.

'It's too late to help any now, isn't it, Jethro?' she said.

'That's what I'd say,' he agreed. 'If we'd been here sooner—'

Lucy and Clyde ran into the room.

'It's my pastor!' Lucy cried, throwing herself upon Reverend Bigbee. 'What have you done to him? You've murdered him! That's what you've done!'

Clyde tried to lift Lucy, but she clung to Reverend Bigbee.

'What were you doing here in this house, Reverend Bigbee?' she said, turning and looking accusingly at Molly.

'He came here looking for Christine,' Molly said calmly, 'and when he found out that she'd eloped, he came in here and cut his arm with that piece of broken glass.'

'That's a lie!' Lucy cried. 'You murdered him yourself! You got him to come here and then murdered him!'

'I did not!'

'You did too!'

'He was looking for Christine—that's what caused it.'

'Where's Mrs. Bigbee?' Lucy said.

'I told you she'd eloped. She ran away with a man.'

Lucy fainted and fell backward on the floor. Clyde picked her up and carried her to the bed. Molly and Lily got a towel and some water and tried to revive her.

While they were working over Lucy, Doc Logan came in. He looked first at Reverend Bigbee's body on the floor and then at Lucy Trotter.

'What's the matter here?' he said.

Molly spun round on her heels at the sound of his voice. 'I told you not to phone for Doc Logan, Lily!' she said angrily. 'I told you to get somebody else!'

'I was so excited I couldn't think of anybody else, Mama,' she said. 'Please don't be angry.'

Doc examined Reverend Bigbee and then got up and looked at Lucy.

'You'd better take her home and keep her quiet, Clyde,' he said. 'I'll give you some pills she should take an hour apart until you can get her asleep.' He opened his satchel and shook half a dozen small white pills into an envelope. Then he went back to Reverend Bigbee's body. 'There's nothing I can do,' he said. 'There's been too much loss of blood.'

Clyde carried Lucy from the room and started home with her. Doc turned to Jethro.

'The thing to do is notify his wife and phone for the undertaker,' he told Jethro. Jethro glanced inquiringly at Molly. 'Where can I wash my hands?'

Jethro led him to the kitchen. Molly and Lily walked behind them.

'Mrs. Bigbee ought to be notified right away,' Doc said, looking over his shoulder while he washed his hands at the sink. 'Molly, maybe that's something you should do.'

'Christine Bigbee ran away tonight, Doc,' she told him. 'That's what caused all this. He came here looking for her, and when he found out Christine and Benny Ballard ran away, he did that to himself.'

'I'll be damned,' Doc said, puzzled. 'I never would have thought she'd do anything like that.'

He dried his hands on a towel Jethro handed him.

'Who is this Benny Ballard?' he asked.

'He's a very high-class gentleman, Doc. I'd have gone off with him myself, if he'd asked me, but he didn't. Christine took to him like hail to a ginhouse roof.'

'Well, I'll be damned!' he said, shaking his head. 'These things sure do crop up in the most unexpected places. I'd never have thought that Reverend Bigbee's wife would run away like that.' He smiled at Lily and walked over to where she was standing and put his arm around her. 'Where've you been keeping yourself lately, Lily?' he said, bending over her intimately. 'It's been a long, long time since I've seen you.' He gave her a tight hug. 'It's been too long, Lily.'

Lily smiled up at him before turning to look at her mother's expressionless face.

Chapter 18

I T was after midnight when Lily and Perry rode up in the elevator to their room on the tenth floor of the hotel. For the third successive day since leaving home they had been sitting in motion-picture theatres from the time the doors opened at nine-thirty in the morning until the last show was over at midnight. That day they had seen five different double-feature shows, and had sat through one of them twice, because Lily had said she wanted to see the part about the horseback trip over the mountain again.

Lily was ecstatic. There was only one movie theatre in Agricola and it changed programmes only twice a week and she had never before had an opportunity to see as many movies as she wanted to.

'Isn't it simply wonderful, Perry?' she said excitedly when they were in their room. She sat down on the side of the bed and tapped her feet on the floor as though keeping time to music. 'I feel just like a beautiful flower that's opening up its delicate petals in the warm sunshine and getting ready to blossom for the first time. It's so marvellous that a thrill goes all through me every time I think about it. Don't you think it's marvellous to see all the movies we want to, Perry? I could go to them for ever and never get tired. Doesn't it make you feel so alive and tingly, Perry? I feel a thrill running through me every minute. I never want to leave here and go back to that old slow-poke Agricola again. I just couldn't stand that dreary old place with only two movies a week, after this. Could you, Perry?'

Perry's eyes were hurting and he felt light-headed and dizzy. He had had sharp pains in his head since ten o'clock that morning. During the final show that evening the screen had become so blurred that he had not been able to comprehend what the picture was about.

'Oh, I just think it's too thrilling for words,' Lily said, getting up and walking around the room. 'I don't feel like the same old me any more.' She kicked off her slippers and began to undress, scattering her garments on the floor. 'Have you ever in your life seen anybody so thrilling as Gene Autry when he smiles, Perry? I wish he'd sweep me off my feet and make love to me. Isn't he divine?' When she finished undressing, she went to the mirror and brushed her hair energetically. 'And, Perry, do you remember in that picture where Rita Hayworth had such a terrible time holding the man she loved? I actually ached to reach out and do something to help her. It was heartbreaking to sit there and not be able to do a thing to make him realize how wonderful life would be with her. The poor thing! I actually died when he left her for that dowdy creature he picked up at the races! Wouldn't Gene Autry and Rita Hayworth make marvellous lovers? I wonder if they know that? Somebody ought to tell them right away while they're still young. Don't you think I look like Rita Hayworth? We have the same type of figure that simply makes men go wild about us, don't we, Perry? We both have the same dreamy eyes, don't we, Perry?' She stepped back, placing one hand on her hip, and looked at herself approvingly in the mirror. 'I'm so glad we came,' she said, posing rigidly. 'I was afraid at first it was a silly thing to do, but now I think it's the most wonderful thing that ever happened to me. I wouldn't have missed it for anything! It's just too marvellous for words!'

With a running leap she jumped into bed. Before Perry could turn out the lights, she reached to the table and got a stack of comic magazines she had made him buy her. She had read dozens of the comics since they got there, and Perry had been unable to interest her in anything else when they were not at the movies. When they left home on the bus, Lily had promised Perry she would marry him right away. The first thing they did was to find a place to stay, but after they had registered at the hotel it was too late to get the marriage licence that day. The next morning Lily made Perry take her into the first movie they passed on their way to the marriage licence bureau, and from that time on he had not been able to persuade her to stop going to the movies or reading comic magazines long enough to apply for the licence. In addition to that, Perry was constantly worried about their staying together in the same room, even though they had registered as Mr. and Mrs. Perry Trotter, when they were not actually married. He was certain that the police would break down the door of their room any minute and arrest them both.

Perry got into bed and moved as close as he could to Lily while she read the comics. Besides everything else on his mind, he was worried about money. When they left home, he had taken all his savings from the bank, and he knew at the time that he had barely enough for their return bus tickets after paying for the marriage licence and staying at the hotel for two nights. As it was, Lily had made him spend so much money for movies and comic magazines that he did not have enough money left to pay their hotel bill, much less buy bus tickets. He knew he would have to telephone his father and ask for some money before they could leave, and he had waited as long as he could before doing that because he knew his father would ask whether he and Lily were married. His mother would make things even worse if he had to call her on the phone, but he hoped to avoid that by calling his father at the planing mill. He had told Lily several times that they were almost broke, but it had made no impression on her.

He lay beside Lily for the next hour, hoping every minute she would put the comics aside. Every once in a while she would laugh at something she was reading in the comics and snuggle closer against the pillow. Twice he got up to get a drink of water, each time crawling over her instead of getting out on his side of the bed, but he was still unable to distract her attention. Finally, with his head dizzy with shooting pains, he fell asleep.

The next morning Perry awoke before Lily and hurriedly got up and dressed. She was still asleep when he tiptoed from the room and went downstairs to the lobby to phone his father at the planing mill in Agricola.

Just as he had feared, the first thing Clyde asked was whether he and Lily were married. Perry pretended not to be able to hear him clearly. Clyde asked the question a second time, the words blasting loudly against his ear. Perry made a mumbling reply.

'Mighty glad to hear from you, son,' his father shouted at

him. 'How's it feel to be a married man? Feel any different now than you did before?'

He could think of no way to evade the question any longer and he realized his father would have to know sooner or later. While Clyde was shouting about something else, Perry decided he might as well tell his father the truth and get it over with.

'Dad, something's gone wrong,' he said preliminarily.

'What went wrong?'

'It hasn't worked out right, yet.'

'What hasn't worked out?'

'We haven't been married, yet,' he said fearfully.

'Haven't done what?'

'Haven't got married, yet.'

'Why not?' Clyde shouted. 'What in hell have you been doing up there all this time?'

'Nothing much.'

'Nothing much!' he said. 'Why haven't you? Didn't you and Lily run away to get married? Wasn't that what you went for? It's the damnedest thing I ever heard of. What're you waiting for?'

'Lily says she's not ready yet.'

'Not ready yet!' his father yelled over the phone. 'What does it take to get her ready—wasn't she ready when she ran away with you?'

'I thought she was, Dad.'

'What's the matter with her then?'

'She won't say, Dad. I don't know what it is.'

Clyde said nothing right away. Perry listened to the buzzing sound that hummed in his ear while he waited to hear what his father would say next.

'Did you understand what I said, Dad?' he asked.

'I heard you but I don't understand it.'

'She just won't do it, Dad. I can't make her.'

'Are you and her staying together, anyway?'

'Yes, sir,' he answered in a trembling voice.

'Well, what in hell's wrong then?'

'She wants to go to the movies all the time, and then when we get back to the hotel, she reads the comics—'

'Does what?'

163

'Reads the funnies all the time in bed.'

'Say that again, son,' his father said in a faraway voice. 'I don't think I heard you right the first time.'

'She reads the funnies—the comic magazines—like *Secret Agent Jack* and *Confidential Secretary*—like they sell at the drugstore for a dime.'

There was a long silence.

'What should I do, Dad?' Perry asked in a pleading voice.

'It's got me stumped,' Clyde admitted. 'I don't know what you can do with a woman like that. I've never run across one like her before. It's all new to me. There's no way of knowing what this younger generation's up to. Maybe she's planning a big wedding, or something like that.'

'She doesn't act like she's planning any kind of wedding,' Perry said in a thin voice. 'She just acts like she's a fool about the movies and the comics.'

'The only thing I can think of offhand is to hide her clothes so she can't go out to those God damn picture shows. That might help. I don't know.'

'She'd still read the comics in bed all the time,' Perry said, 'but it might help some. I'll try it, anyway.' He stopped for a moment. 'Does Mama know?'

'Of course she knows,' Clyde told him. 'At least she thinks she knows. She thinks you and Lily got married right away when you ran off. God only knows what she'd say if she knew you hadn't got married yet. You know how your mother is.'

'You won't tell her something's gone wrong, will you, Dad?'

'I won't tell her a thing, but you'd better get busy and get married before she finds it out.'

'I'll try hard, Dad,' Perry promised. Then he added desperately, 'I'm all out of money, Dad. Could you send me a little right away?'

'I'll see what I can do,' Clyde told him.

'Please don't wait too long, Dad, because I've spent nearly all I had.'

After leaving the telephone booth, Perry got into the elevator and went up to the room. Lily was still asleep, and he hastily gathered up her clothes and hid them between the dresser and the wall. When he was certain all of her things were out of sight, he sat down on the bed. Lily awoke slowly. She looked at the ceiling through partly open eyes for several moments and then raised her head and looked at the bright sunlight shining through the windows. After that she sat up and propped herself against the pillows.

'Hello, Perry,' she said casually, barely glancing at him as she reached down to the floor and picked up a handful of magazines.

'Lily, let's hurry and eat breakfast so we can go get the licence,' he pleaded.

She thumbed through one of the magazines until she found the page she was looking for.

'Gee-whiz, Lily, don't you ever want to get married at all?' he said, putting his hand on her. 'You said we'd get married as soon as we got here. Don't you want to at all any more? Don't you think we ought to?'

'There's oodles of time, Perry,' she said, pushing his hand from her. 'There's no need to hurry. I like it this way. I feel just like Rita Hayworth when she woke up and found that horrid man had left her sometime during the night after she'd positively given him her very soul. It's times like that when we women suffer pure agony. It leaves a big hollow feeling deep down inside you, Perry, and you just can't think of anything else. Of course you're as mad as a hornet at him, but you'd do anything in the world for him if he'd only come back and take you into his arms. That's exactly how I feel, Perry. It's such a marvellous thrill.'

He snatched the comic from her hands and threw it across the room. Lily jumped out of bed. She stamped her feet angrily and beat her clenched fists together.

'Just for that, Perry Trotter, I won't tell you when I'll get married! I may change my mind and never get married now! Why do you have to go and spoil everything!'

She walked round the room looking for her clothes.

'Please don't be like that, Lily,' he begged.

'It's time to go to the movies.'

'I'm never going to another movie as long as I live,' he stated defiantly. 'I'm through going to those things. I've had enough.'

'You can stay here, Perry, and I'll go by myself,' she told him curtly and then got down on her knees and looked under the bed. 'Where are my clothes, Perry Trotter?'

Perry ignored her question and went to the window and looked down at the street. He had been standing there for only a short time when she caught his arm and jerked him around.

'You give me my clothes this very instant, Perry Trotter!' she cried. 'I won't stand for this. Do you hear me, Perry Trotter!'

Perry had been determined to follow his father's advice, and he wondered what his father would do under the circumstances. Lily was impatiently tapping her foot on the floor.

'Lily—' he said pleadingly, going to her and trying to put his arms around her. She pushed him away before he could touch her. 'Please, Lily—'

'I'm waiting for you to do as I told you, Perry Trotter,' she said with firm determination. 'You're not going to take my clothes and keep me from going to the movies.'

He tried to think what his father would do now, but it was difficult to imagine seeing his father confronted by Lily and demanding that he give her back her clothes. She stood there defiantly while he tried to think what he could do. He wanted to put his arms around her and plead with her, but when he moved closer, her arm was thrust against his chest and he found himself stumbling backward.

After that he went to the dresser and pulled it away from the wall. Her clothes fell into a heap upon the floor and he picked them up and carried them to her. Lily snatched them from his hands and turned her back while she dressed. Perry sat down on the foot of the bed and watched dejectedly. She spent several minutes combing and setting her hair, and when that was finished, she picked up her purse and went to the door.

'How are you going to get into those movies?' he asked her.

Lily stopped with her hand on the knob.

'You don't have enough money to get into all those shows,' he said with a feeling of confidence. 'They won't let you in free.'

She opened her purse calmly. They both knew that she had no money in it.

'I'll get in some way,' she said with a fleeting smile. She then walked out of the room and slammed the door behind her.

Perry was stunned. He did not know what to do. It had not occurred to him that she would actually walk out and leave him, whether she had enough money for the movies or not. It was ten o'clock then, and it would be midnight before she came back. Then it occurred to him that she might not come back at all. He opened the door and ran down the hall to the elevator. When he got there, she had already gone down to the lobby, and he began ringing the elevator bell. It was several minutes before an elevator stopped at the floor, and by the time he reached the lobby she was nowhere within sight. He ran to the street, looking frantically at the faces in the crowds. After a while he began walking aimlessly, hoping that somehow he would be able to find her before she went into one of the movies.

He gave up at dark, tired and hungry, and started back to the hotel. He had walked all day, going from one movie theatre to another and watching the crowds enter and leave, and he hoped that either she would be waiting for him at the hotel or that she had left a message for him.

When he unlocked the door and stepped into the room, one of the lights was burning, and for a moment he was sure Lily was there. Then a man and a woman, who had been standing against the wall, stepped forward and surrounded him. The man was about the same age as his father and the woman appeared to be about forty. Both were grim and unsmiling. The man was standing between him and the door to prevent him from reaching it.

'Is your name Perry Trotter?' the strange man asked.

'Yes, sir,' Perry replied through trembling lips.

'Pack up your clothes. You're going home.'

'But, Lily—' he said. 'I can't leave Lily—'

'She's not going,' the woman said, speaking for the first time.

'Not going?' Perry said. 'How do you know? Have you seen her?'

The woman nodded. 'She won't be able to go,' she said kindly. 'There's been some trouble. She'll have to stay here for a while.'

'What kind of trouble? What did Lily do?'

Neither of them answered him. He tried to swallow, but he found it was too difficult and he almost choked. He glanced at the strange man's unsmiling face and then back at the motherly looking woman.

'What did Lily do?' he asked again as he felt warm tears filling his eyes. 'Why does she have to stay here?'

'Because she said she'd run away again if we took her home.'

'But all she wanted was to go to the movies,' he protested. 'She's crazy about movies and the comics.'

'I know,' the woman said as she patted him gently on the shoulder, 'but she shouldn't be on the streets asking strangers to take her to the movies. Now, you'd better pack up your things so we can start, Perry.'

Chapter 19

T HERE had been a warm drizzly shower in mid-afternoon and the sun was shining from a clear blue sky when the three Negroes carried the last piece of furniture from the truck and, under Molly's direction, placed it in its proper position in the house. Now that everything was done, she sank wearily into a chair and gazed with satisfaction at the parlour and its furnishings. Molly had hung curtains over the windows, placed the tall blue china vase on the centre table, and put the hat tree in the corner behind the door. The red sofa, looking worn and shabby in its new surroundings, was nevertheless comfortable and inviting in appearance. An ornate glass chandelier hanging from the ceiling, which had been left behind at Jamie Denton's insistence by the previous renters, added a touch of splendour and elegance to the parlour. Molly had done everything she could think of to make the room have a cheerful homelike atmosphere and she was proud of what she had accomplished in a day's time. From where she sat, she could look through the window and see the bright afternoon sun shining on the house next door. It was a dilapidated, unpainted, frame dwelling with a rusty tin roof. Some of the windows had been broken and boarded up, and a rank growth of pigweeds reached almost to the level of the porch. The whole neighbourhood was weedgrown and uncared for. The streets were unpaved and potted with mud holes that never quite dried up the year around. The vacant lots were piled with heaps of rubbish, tin cans, and rusting automobile bodies that children had converted into playhouses. The railroad tracks were only a hundred feet away, and the fifteen or twenty freight cars that were always on the sidings provided the only view that could be seen from the front porches. Many of the houses had *Men Only* signs nailed to them, a few had crudely lettered *Guests* signs, and some of the others were identified, just as Molly's house was, by a small enamelled *Rooms for Rent* sign. The street, which was only three blocks long, was known as Big Sal's Hollow. Big Sal Humphrey had been the first to move there and keep an open house and, although she had been dead for several years, the name remained. In her time Big Sal was known all over Cherokee County for being the first to provide Saturday afternoon matinees especially for farmers from the country who wanted to visit her house but who had to be home by dark to milk the cows and to feed and water their stock. There were always a few men in the Hollow every evening, but the large crowds came on Saturday nights, and from sundown to four or five o'clock in the morning the street was filled with boisterous men and boys, many of whom got drunk before the evening was over and fell into the mud holes. From time to time one of the women's clubs or auxiliaries held indignation meetings and made the mayor close up the houses and run the girls out of town, but after a week or two the resorts opened again and the girls drifted back and nothing was done about it for a year or so when another delegation called on the mayor.

Molly closed her eyes and was dozing when a loud noise in the hall awoke her with a start. She sat up and looked around. Jamie Denton, his bony body stooped with the weight of a large framed painting, came into the parlour. The picture he was partly carrying and partly dragging was about five feet long and four feet high and it had a heavy gilt frame around it. Jamie dragged the picture across the room and leaned it against the centre table. Then he stepped back, wiping the perspiration from his face, and took a good look at the painting in its new surroundings. Molly, still too surprised to say anything, leaned forward. Jamie turned to her with a wide satisfied grin.

'Ain't that something, Mrs. Bowser?' he commented proudly. 'Ain't it though?'

Molly nodded enthusiastically, but still a little puzzled.

'I had to take that in payment of rent once,' he said pausing to take a deep breath, 'and I got to thinking about it and decided

170

the thing to do was make a present of it to you. I don't know nobody else in Agricola who'd appreciate it like you would, because it sort of goes along with you, and besides I'd like to see you get off to a good start.'

Jamie pulled up a chair and sat down where he could look at the picture and rest at the same time. The oil painting was dusty and in need of cleaning, but the life-size figure of a heavily proportioned young woman, who was reclining on her elbow while she held a daisy to her nose and coyly smelled it, was evocative and arresting.

'Is she one of your former wives in her younger days, Mr. Denton?' Molly asked him.

'She's no relation of mine,' Jamie replied indignantly. 'I wouldn't stand for having no wife of mine laying around the house with no clothes on like that and smelling daisies. But,' he added tolerantly, 'I wouldn't raise no objections to it otherwise.'

'Whoever she is she's beautiful,' Molly said, sighing wistfully. 'I sure wish I looked like her. I don't blame her for having her picture painted and hung on the wall. I wouldn't hesitate to have my own likeness painted if I looked half as good as her.'

'It does look mighty nice, now don't it?' Jamie crossed his legs and swung his free foot. 'I had that stored away in my closet, but I hardly ever looked at it and it didn't do nobody no good stuck away out of sight like that, and so I got to thinking and figured if you was to hang it on your parlour wall down there a lot of lonesome folks would admire and benefit by it. On top of that, when a man walks in and sees a picture like that right off, it sort of makes him feel at home without more ado.'

Jamie got up and hung the painting on a nail somebody had driven into the bare pine-boarded wall. After carefully straightening it, he went to the other side of the room and sat down on the sofa where he could admire it in comfort.

'You've sure got a nice homey place here, Mrs. Bowser,' he told her, looking around the parlour and nodding with approval. 'It's a heap nicer for you down here than that other house out on Muscadine Street. There's a lot of lonesome men in the world who've got nowhere to turn and they appreciate having somebody like you to provide a nice homey place they can go to. It's just like I always tell Fred Thurston when he says he wants to run for re-election for mayor again and worries about the votes in those women's auxiliaries. I tell him it takes all kinds of people to make a world and that we couldn't get along without the good women no more than we could get along without the ones who live down here in the Hollow. Of course the fact that I own and rent out all the houses down here don't have nothing to do with it. It's all on account of my civic spirit that I want to see everybody satisfied.'

'I need a new carpet pretty bad,' Molly said, rubbing the toe of her shoe over a threadbare spot in the blue floor covering. 'This old thing looks worse than ever, now that that fine picture's hanging on the wall.' She took a deep breath. 'I can't do everything all at once, though. A new carpet'll have to wait a while.'

'It'll come,' Jamie assured her. 'It'll come in time.' He stopped looking at the painting and glanced at the arrangement of furniture in the room. 'I always believe in doing first things first, and getting moved down here to the South Side was the big task to get done and out of the way. It was a nice clean quick job, but I knowed it wouldn't be no trouble, once we up and started. The worst part about moving is thinking how hard it's going to be beforehand. Once it's over, it don't seem like it was hard at all.' He stopped and watched Molly's expression for a moment. 'Now that it's all done and finished, I hope there ain't no hard feelings between us, Mrs. Bowser. I believe in forgiving and forgetting, and I want to do my share of it. That little spat we had a while back—that ain't rankling you none now, is it, Mrs. Bowser?'

Molly shook her head. 'It doesn't bother me at all now, Mr. Denton, since I resigned myself. It's all in the past and clean forgotten.'

'I'm sure glad to hear you say that,' he said with relief. 'If there's one thing I don't like, it's having somebody hold a grudge against me. It makes collecting the rent a heap harder to do, too.'

'I reckon I did act a little hasty that time and let my mind speak out for itself before I could put a stop to it, but the whole trouble was I was getting desperate. Now that I've decided to let Jethro stay around, I'm calm and peaceful. As long as a woman's got a man of some sort handy, she quits losing her head over little things. Jethro's a poor excuse for a man, but

172

he'll have to do. I decided I'd better go ahead and take him while I could before some other desperate woman got hold of him. I lost out getting the kind of man I wanted, but I'm big enough to admit it.'

'Where's Jethro now? I didn't see him around when I came in a little while ago.'

'Oh, he's out back somewhere. He was poking in those big trash piles out there the last time I noticed him.'

The sun had set and it was dark enough at last to turn on the lights. Molly got up and pulled down the shades. She had been waiting all afternoon for the time to come when she could see the chandelier in all its glory. With trembling hand she turned the switch. A dazzling display of light burst upon the room. Dozens of iridescent cut-glass figures of cupids and mermaids were suspended from the chandelier on invisible threads, and the slightest disturbance of the air started them twisting and turning. Slivers of reflected light danced on the walls and ceiling, and the huge oil painting came to life in the bright illumination.

'I've always wanted to live in a house with beautiful things like these,' she said as she clasped and unclasped her hands over and over again. 'This's almost too good to be true. I can hardly believe this's me looking at it. It's like—like—fairyland, Mr. Denton!'

While they watched the display of light, Geraldine and Dixie Lee came down the hall and stopped and looked at the chandelier in wonder. The two girls had rented rooms that afternoon while Molly was still busy arranging furniture and had moved in immediately. Geraldine, a small slender girl with blue-black hair, was the younger of the two. She said she was eighteen, but she did not appear to be more than fifteen or sixteen. Dixie Lee, who was blonde, and talkative, was twenty.

'That's the prettiest thing I ever saw, Mrs. Bowser,' Dixie Lee said from the doorway. 'It's lovely.'

'Isn't it, though?' Molly said enthusiastically. 'I'm real proud of it.'

'Could we come in sometime and just sit and look at it, Mrs. Bowser?'

'Of course,' she told them. 'I want everybody to enjoy it. I wouldn't think of keeping it all to myself.'

While Molly and Dixie Lee had been talking, Jamie had picked up his hat and was moving cautiously toward the door. There was a frightened look on his face and his hands were shaking. Molly reached out and caught him by the arm.

'Don't leave so soon, Mr. Denton,' she said, trying to pull him away from the door. 'It's early yet. I was thinking of having a little celebration, and you'd appreciate what I had planned for you, Mr. Denton. I want to treat you to a good time, and it won't cost you a dime, neither. I'll bet it's been a long time since you've had a really truly good time. Come back to the sofa and sit down for a while and talk to Dixie Lee or Geraldine.' She turned and beckoned to Geraldine.

'Nope, I couldn't do that,' Jamie said, shaking his head. 'I've got to go right away. Can't stay another minute.'

'But the girls want to get acquainted with you, Mr. Denton. Wouldn't you like to know them better? They're really truly likeable young ladies, Mr. Denton.'

He pulled himself from Molly's grasp and ran past Geraldine. Dixie Lee was still standing in the doorway, and when he found himself confronted by her, he ducked his head and stooped over. He got past her before she could stop him.

'That's the most ungrateful man I ever saw,' Molly said bitterly. 'I was going to be big-hearted to him, too.'

While they were listening to the sound of Jamie running across the back porch, somebody came through the front door. Molly was tucking away some loose strands of hair behind her ears when Clyde Trotter walked into the parlour.

'What's this?' he said, gaping at the chandelier. 'Looks like the circus has come to town.'

'Isn't it beautiful, Clyde?' Molly said proudly.

'I never saw a sight like that before in my life Molly, how did you get your place fixed up like this? It sure puts that shack up on Muscadine Street in the shade.'

'Oh, I just worked at it, Clyde.'

He walked over to the oil painting and looked at it closely for a long time. While he was standing with his back to the room, Molly motioned for Geraldine and Dixie to leave. It was several minutes before he could turn away from it. Molly had already seated herself on the sofa and was waiting for him.

'Have you heard anything, Clyde?' she asked anxiously.

Clyde sat down on the sofa.

'Perry called me on the phone this morning,' he said. 'That's what I dropped in to tell you about, Molly.'

'Are they married? When are they coming home?'

'That's what I don't know, for sure. Perry said Lily's been going to the movies so much they haven't had time to get the licence. That's what he said this morning, and from the way he talked it didn't sound to me like they'd do anything about it for a while, anyway.'

'Lily always was crazy about the movies,' Molly said with an understanding nod. 'I'm not a bit surprised.' She clasped and unclasped her hands time after time. 'I did the best thing I could think of—for Lily's sake—when I put Perry up to running away with her. I was desperate, Clyde. I knew what was going to become of me, and that made me as certain as the sun rises on Wednesday morning what would happen to her if she stayed here. It was the last chance to save her—from me. If I could raise her all over again, I could save her myself. But it's too late now.' She began to cry. Tears filled her eyes. 'It's awful to be like me and not be able to change. It's awful to know you've done something wrong and not be able to undo it. I hope there're not many women like me in the world, but if there are I sure can sympathize with every last one of them. Poor Lily! She was such a sweet child! I wish I was dead!'

'Maybe they'll get married yet, Molly,' Clyde said uneasily. 'Let's wait and see before you get so upset about it.'

'It's all my fault,' she said as she covered her face with her hands. 'I'm to blame, and God's punishing me for my sins just like Lucy said—and now I couldn't even stop being what I am if I tried. If Lily comes back, I won't be able to send her away. I know I should—but I won't. I even fixed up a room for her this afternoon—and I shouldn't have done that!'

Neither of them spoke for a long time. Molly, still sobbing, dried her tears on the hem of her skirt and got up.

'Lucy was dead right, Clyde,' she said. 'Lucy told me the sure hand of God would lead me to where I am now, and it did.'

'Lucy's got a queer streak in her, Molly. She picked on you

175

because you were friendly with Christine Bigbee. She had the notion that God intended for her to be a minister's wife, and that Christine and I—and you, too—had conspired with the devil to keep her from being married to Reverend Bigbee. Sometimes I'd have given my right arm if she was married to him instead of to me, but it's too late now.'

'If she's satisfied to see me down here in the Hollow now, I guess I can be, too,' Molly said. 'Maybe it's for the best, after all. I feel more at home down here than I ever did anywhere else, and maybe it's where I belonged all the time. If it hadn't been for Lily—' She paused in the doorway and looked back. 'I've got a jug of wine in the kitchen. You'll stay, won't you, Clyde—for old time's sake?'

Clyde, looking down at the floor, nodded.

DATE DUE